Run With the Hunted 4: VIP
By Jennifer R. Donohue

Run with the Hunted 4: VIP © 2021 by Jennifer R. Donohue

Paperback ISBN: 9781945548161
Ebook ISBN: 9781945548154

For Jim

Chapter One

Nobody at this party matters, but I thought it would be amusing to attend anyway. I've been to the club hosting it before, and know the degree to which I should dress. No red soles tonight; far too showy and that would strike the wrong note with other guests. I needn't draw *too* much attention, and not the sort which would generate resentment.

The lighting is dim, kind to everybody's faces even before things become drink-blurred. Drink-blurred for them, that is; I have a firm grip on sobriety, sometimes in spite of how much alcohol I've consumed. Some genetic luck, though if I'd been the type to *want* to imbibe to excess, it would certainly be a burden; instead, it was a boon in my earlier days, when every penny counted. But there is a distinct benefit to being the most sober one in the room, or at a table, especially if deals are being made, or if the people with you have nefarious intentions. Which isn't to say that I always assume the worst of people, you understand, it's just necessary to keep your wiles about you while also matching the proper mood for the environment.

They have champagne so I have a champagne cocktail; there's just something about the aesthetic of holding a champagne flute that is so compelling. There is some small talk to be had, in the way of these things, and at about the middle of the evening, if my estimation is correct, i find myself standing next to a man who really doesn't seem as though he fits well here.

"What are we celebrating?" he asks me, nodding to my champagne flute. It's another reason I almost always get champagne, it gives people a chance to ask me that and feel clever.

"I'm not certain yet," I say, with my head tilted just so. He is handsome, and his suit fits him particularly well. There's something about how he holds himself, though, that tells me a suit is not his preferred manner of dress. "I simply had the impulse."

"Maybe you're celebrating our meeting," he says, a little bold I think. But his demeanor says that he doesn't do this often, and he is trying very hard to be earnest, so I think I will give him the benefit of the doubt for now.

"I suppose that remains to be seen," I say, and smile. As I take the next sip of my cocktail, I drop my eyes to his shoes, which are cowboy boots made of some exotic leather; I'm not entirely sure, with this lighting, but my guess is ostrich. Oh very interesting; something to tell Dolly about later, when I'm making the girls listen to my tales of the evening, if I have any tales of this evening. I did not, until this point.

"I suppose it does," he says. "Well let me grab my own whatever that is…?"

"Ask them for a champagne cocktail."

"A champagne cocktail, and then we can go to one of those tables there, and we'll see how things progress?" He smiles a little quizzically, as though the champagne cocktail were not simply called that, but one could excuse him for not knowing. I'd guess that he prefers beers, probably lagers. Maybe stouts.

"Perhaps you'd prefer a black velvet," I say. "There *is* still champagne involved, I promise."

"Perhaps," he says, like he's tasting the word. "I'll be right back with one of those then. Do you need a top off?"

"Not right now, thank you." He moves easily through the crowd, comfortable with himself despite the suit, and has the kind of presence where people kind of move for him, he isn't jostled or jostling. I watch his face in the bar mirror; he smiles easily for the server, slides a cash tip across the bar when he receives his drink, also giving a little nod. When he turns back around, he meets my eyes across the room and raises his glass a little, champagne with stout layered on top. Then he nods towards the tables, and we each cross the room to meet there; I pause briefly to speak with somebody I recognize from a previous party, and when we part I have a mental note to drop a missive to Marquis. Sooner or later, they're going to soften again; it just isn't in their nature to make me keep *groveling*.

"Thank you for the drink recommendation, miss," he says. He'd sampled it by the time I reached the table, the layers starting to lose their distinction. "Just champagne is definitely a little too sweet for my taste."

"You struck me as a beer aficionado," I say. "I'm pleased I was right."

"What gave me away?"

"Your boots."

"My boots?" He's the sort of man who's cultivated an easy smile in place of a whole myriad of emotions, such as surprise and disappointment and confusion. "My best boots outed me as a beer drinker?"

"They are western boots. Ostrich western boots."

"They are at that." He leans back in his seat a little, straightens his leg out to admire them. "You don't see a lot of these in places like this, I guess."

"I do not." I don't see many ostrich leather accoutrements in general, or perhaps not in North America, but I needn't inform him of that. "They suit you, though. You're obviously comfortable."

"Well thank you, I am." We nod at each over the rims of our glasses. What an interesting flirtation this is, because he does not seem actually interested in flirting, but he has something he is working around to. He sets his drink down, starts to lean his elbows on the table, just in repose, but something that isn't manners hitches him up and he thinks better of it. Which is not to say I think he's unmannerly, but it's a physical inhibition, new or he wouldn't have forgotten it.

"Except for that," I say mildly, and there's that smile again, a rueful tilt of the head.

"Except for that." He considers a moment, shakes his head. "Alright, I might as well just lay things out, I'm not good at social games. I've got kind of a proposition, and I'd like you to hear me out." He sees my face and holds up his hands just a little, right above the table's surface. "Proposition's the wrong word. It's a job offer."

I take one last sip of my champagne before I set it down, rearrange myself slightly in my seat. "Perhaps, before I hear you out, we ought to ascertain just who you think I am?" I was not expecting a job offer, nor had I heard of this man from any of my contacts, and I feel certain I would have, were they sending him my way. The chances of a job just dropping from the heavens into my lap at rather a boring, inconsequential party were...low. Goodness, have I just been mistaken for an escort? "Just to keep from wasting your time, of course."

He repeats the raised hands gesture, like he wants to gentle the situation. "I hope I haven't offended you, I saw you and thought I recognized you, but I don't really know where. Like maybe I'd seen your face in the paper for a local theater concern that just wrapped up production."

"And you'd like to hire an actress privately?" He doesn't seem to be lying; nor does he seem to be telling the truth, and I am amused and intrigued.

"Actually yes. It's real weird, and a little complicated, and I don't blame you one bit if you say no."

"Well now I absolutely *must* hear you out," I say, smiling. "Though lest I mislead you further, I am not said stage actress, and I daresay we've until this point never shared a space."

"Oh," he said, actually crestfallen, the darling. "Well I'm sorry to have bothered—"

I reach out and touch his wrist as he starts to get up. "You haven't bothered me, this is one of the most dull parties I had ever been to until you approached."

"Really?"

I nod. "Cross my heart."

He has some more of his drink, maybe to collect his thoughts after having been so swiftly derailed. He is clearly used to other, perhaps more physical, kinds of challenges. "I find myself in need of a wife," he says finally, and I get the sense that he had a different sort of speech planned. "And I'm not in the business of propositioning beautiful women that I meet in clubs, and I'm not interested in making women do anything they don't want to. But I was in different circumstances, which have changed, and I have a legal deadline coming up, so I don't have the time to do things the right way."

I certainly had not expected anything of that sort. "So in order to meet this legal deadline, you wanted to hire an actress to be your wife?" I ask. "What sort of a legal deadline?"

"One my parents set, for a trust. See, me and my brother were both happy to just do our own thing and live on a stipend and get married on our own time." Oh a *trust*. There are such fascinating rules surrounding those. I don't know many lawyers, but at least one in my acquaintance has been a trust lawyer, and the *stories* he could tell.

"You said your circumstances changed, though. What were you and your brother up to?"

"Bull riding, actually," he said, and that's where his easy physicality comes from. I'm not certain I've ever known a bull rider, and Dolly's escapades at bars with sawdust on the floor do not count. "But I wrecked my shoulder and elbow just about for good pretty recently, and can't do that anymore, but my brother still can."

"So you were going to both just take the stipend, but since you cannot continue with what you were doing..."

"I thought I'd make a go of it, yeah."

"May I ask what the trust is...regarding?" I'm not even certain how to phrase it.

"Oh yeah, sure. My family's one of the biggest ostrich farming concerns in North America."

"Oh I see." I could just imagine Dolly's excitement. A bull rider *and* an ostrich farmer, she will be simply obsessed. She'll throttle me, if I turn this down. A business marriage, so a man who can no longer bull ride might access his family's fortunes.

"And how long are you envisioning this whirlwind courtship and subsequent marriage needing to last?"

He laughs, open and honest; he's amazed and relieved that I haven't thrown my drink in his face and huffed off to have the bouncers remove him. "Oh I don't know, we don't need to break any records like the movie people. The trust doesn't go away if divorce happens."

"Do you have staff that you need to maintain this ruse for?" I have a sudden horror of needing to keep up appearances under the very close scrutiny of his own Mrs. Danvers, and then another thought follows swiftly on the heels of the first. "Besides, I won't do this alone, you understand. For safety's sake."

He frowns a little, but picks up his drink again. Settling into the conversation, the idea that perhaps he has been successful. "I don't know if I follow."

"Well if I'm to be your sudden mysterious and unexpected bride that you might step in and claim your ostrich fortune, I must have my bodyguards with me." I'll have to do something about their clothes, of course, but I do believe it's possible I can get both Bits and Dolly to adopt nice suits in lieu of their riot gear, for this situation. Everything as reinforced and dragon-scaled as can possibly be, of course.

He pauses with his drink midair. "You...have bodyguards?" He looks around, but no bodyguards appear.

I smile indulgently, finish my cocktail. "It's all the rage nowadays."

The poor man looks even more out of his element, but I'm comfortable waiting for him to work through his thoughts. I look out across the room, but the people gathered have become no more interesting in the interim, and no familiar faces have turned up. "There will be some house staff, but nobody's a personal servant, if that's what you mean. And the master suite has enough rooms where behind closed doors, nobody needs to know who's sleeping where."

"That does sound suitable." I study him for a moment; he is a handsome enough man, if a little rugged for my tastes. "How is it that you never found love before now?"

He shrugs. "Just didn't stop long enough, maybe. And not every lady is interested in a bullrider. It's dangerous, and they don't want to go through not knowing if he's going to walk out of the ring at the end of the day." He's been asked this time and again, it seems.

"And your brother is the same way?"

"He's maybe more inclined to accept the advances of a buckle bunny here and there than I ever was, but yeah, I've never yet seen him inclined to settle down. And he knows I want to do this, there's no feud going on."

I raise my eyebrows. "Buckle bunny?"

He clears his throat, hitches in his chair a little. "Slang for women who follow rodeos. Like groupies, but girls of a certain type getting notches on their belts."

"I see." Every industry has its own language, it's just fascinating. And nearly everybody has their own way to denigrate women.

He shakes his head. He's uncomfortable, but I think only because he doesn't want me to think badly of him in that way. "Like I said, I don't get in with all that. And it won't matter anyway, I'm not asking you to perform maritals, just be my wife on paper for long enough to get those things settled. A couple of weeks, probably."

"That seems reasonable." I'm honestly delighted by the whole charade, and he does seem as though he'll behave in a gentlemanly manner. Especially with my 'bodyguards' about; I have seen Dolly put much larger men in their place, when it came to that. But, I cannot accept without consensus, unless I'm also willing to just do the job alone, and I'm not entirely certain that I am. I consider the intersection of bull riding people and ostrich ranching people, and all of that money. "We would need to hash out the events and appearances you anticipate, so that I might be adequately prepared for them. And I need to speak to my associates before I can give you a firm yes, of course."

"Of course," he says. I think he is perhaps marveling that this has worked. I hesitate to speculate what his backup plan may have been. "I'm R.J. Sutter, by the way."

Which of my aliases might be suitable for this? I should have considered sooner. "Madison," I say, and we shake hands, and he looks right into my eyes as we do. He has a warm, firm grip. "May I ask, though, what does the R stand for? I'm not in the habit of calling people by their initials like that."

"If I tell you, does that mean you'll be calling me that?"

"Likely, yes." R.J. *indeed*, my goodness. He very much does not like that, and I can see in his face that he's second guessing everything.

"Rafael," he finally says. "People used to also sometimes call me Rafe."

"Oh darling, that isn't a terrible name at all. I thought you were going to tell me *Ryan* or *Richard* or something." I smile and he laughs, shaking his head.

"No, not Richard." He looks like he wants to ask me something, and I get out my phone before he arrives at a decision.

"Now let's exchange contact information, and I'll tra la la on home and talk to my bodyguards, and I'll be in touch. How does that sound?"

He gets out his phone almost automatically when he sees mine, nodding. "That sounds good."

"Besides, it gives you time to reconsider." His eyes dart up to mine from our screens.

"I'm not sure I can," he says.

Chapter Two

We three don't always live together, but in this particular instance, we've rented a spacious three bedroom apartment on the top floor of a repurposed brick building that used to be I'm not sure what. It isn't quite dire enough for a school or factory, and my curiosity regarding it has only run so deep. There is parking and ensuite laundry and a close proximity of many restaurants which deliver, just beautiful hardwood floors and french doors to let all the light in. I do think Bits has literally boarded the windows in her room, judging from the way she sometimes seems to shrink from the light when she emerges, but Dolly doesn't seem perturbed either way.

Dolly is on the couch with the robot dog when I arrive, watching something which contains a lot of fire and explosions. "Hey Bristles," she says. "I wiped it down first, don't worry. No floor crud on the couch."

"I'm not worried, though perhaps I am concerned. Did you have a security shotgun when you were little, instead of a blanket?" It's difficult for me to understand the robot dog, perhaps because I don't favor animals in general, but also due to its complete lack of physical comfort. One does not *cuddle* a robot dog.

She grins at me. "Doesn't everybody?"

"They do not." I know that she's only needling me, it is her way, but Dolly is astonishingly good at pressing buttons. "I didn't have a security blanket either, I should add."

"No? What'd you have, a security handbag? Actually, I kinda like that, it makes sense. You can whack somebody with a handbag."

"Mmm, no, not that either." I look at her movie, but I don't recognize it, and have no way to assess if it will be over soon. "So I may have a job. Of course I wanted to consult with you girls before accepting out of hand, but I think it sounds both lucrative and interesting. Perhaps a little unusual for us, but we might be able to work an angle."

Without warning she yells "Bitsy! Family meeting!" and turns off the TV. "Bristol, what did you do?"

"*Nothing*, I just told you." Well, if she's already going to be up in arms about it... "I know you've objected to, how do you put it, 'Dolly dress up' in the past, some of it might be required. For both of you. Suits, though, not dresses."

She huffs out a breath while looking at me, and nodding a little, and Bits shuffles out with her hair sticking every which way, VR goggle marks on her face. "We call these family meetings?"

"Got your attention, didn't it?" Dolly grins. "Okay first off we're gonna need suits."

"What? What kind of suits?" Bits blinks at Dolly, blinks at me.

"Dolly, would you please allow me to explain before you hare off on some wild fantasy?"

"You *said*," she says, grinning even more, and I can't help but laugh. She is so incorrigible.

"Yes, I did say suits, but that's only a piece of the job."

"We have a job? Did we talk about this already and I forgot?" Bits sits on the end of Dolly's couch, and the robot dog swivels its head to look at her.

"No, it was brought to me just tonight if you'll let me speak!" I give a little stomp for emphasis, and Dolly sits up straight and folds her hands in her lap. Bits runs a hand through her hair, taming some of its unruliness, and does not comment further. "I was at an otherwise very boring party when a very handsome man asked for my temporary and fraudulent hand in marriage because he has to make an upcoming deadline for a family trust."

Bits blinks some more, and Dolly actually clasps her hands. "This is even better than I could've imagined."

"And I said that I could never take such a job without my bodyguards, and that I must speak to them about it before saying yes."

"And this was a totally normal like, just alcohol party? You didn't have any funny brownies or anything and then read a pulp paperback in a drugstore with a scantily clad lady and/or gentleman on the front before toddling back home again?"

"I had a single glass of champagne," I say icily.

"Just checkin', you understand." I look at her with raised eyebrows and she holds up her hands, not unlike Rafe not so long ago. "Okay, go on. What kind of a trust? Why the hurry, if he's so handsome?"

"Evidently he and his brother were both content with the bull riding circuit, but he's sustained an injury that prevents him from continuing."

"Wait, wait, what's this guy's name?"

I roll my eyes. "He calls himself *R.J.* and I told him that would absolutely not be what I—"

Dolly sits bolt upright. "R.J. Sutter?"

"Oh you know who—"

"And his brother Gabe is having a real good season. Oh wow, Bristles, you've really outdone yourself. Are you even kidding me? R.J. Sutter and you just have no idea."

"And here I thought you'd be pleased that the trust was to do with ostrich farming."

She frowns quizzically. "Why would I be pleased by that?"

"Never mind."

"Look, your husband-to-be—"

"Fake husband-to-be," Bits interjects helpfully. She looks more alert now.

"Thank you, Bitsy. Your unlawfully wedded husband is a two time PBR champion, and for one of those rides, he had 95 points. Actually, I think he got special recognition for that? Maybe the bull got some award that year."

"Okay." Honestly, with all of her vehicle knowledge, and weapons knowledge, and familiarity with both casual and formal violence, I had no idea that Dolly had room for further interests. "This means we would like to accept the job then?" I ask sweetly.

"Hell yes, we would. Right Bits?" Bits nods, reaching over and taking Dolly's popcorn. "Do you think his mechanical bull has a face?"

The rich inner workings of my companions, honestly. "Dolly, darling, I'm sure I have no idea what you're talking about."

"Don't worry about it." She's grinning at her own joke and it's best to just let her have that, I think. I'll call Rafe in the morning to tell him we'll be accepting; it simply wouldn't do to appear too eager. "Okay so you're going to be his mystery bride, people're gonna go *nuts*, the bodyguard idea is a good one actually. We'll have to find somebody who can fit us up in Secret Service dragonscale I guess. I imagine you'll be on that, Bits?"

"Yeah, I'll contact a few people." She looks at me, a little wide eyed. "You're sure this is something you want to do? Fake engaged is one thing, but you'll be really married."

"And then really divorced, yes. It will be fine, it's simply a business arrangement."

"Careful you don't fall for him," Dolly says, taking her popcorn back. "There's movies and country songs and everything about stuff like this."

"Oh goodness, country songs," I say with an elaborate shiver.

"It's a whole culture, Bristol. Keep that in mind, and our bodyguarding'll be easier than not."

"Well, it's a very good thing that I have you to educate me then, isn't it?" I ask, and she makes a face at me as though she realizes, fully, that she invited that. Then another wicked smile surfaces.

"Y'know, it is. And I'm gonna find a bar with a mechanical bull in it so that you're acquainted."

"That will not be necessary..."

"I still just can't get over this. Yeah, I remember now, their family was one of the early adoptors for the ostriches. They used to have I don't even know how many head of cattle before they started reducing, for the carbon, you understand." I nod, because I can follow, but I mostly have no idea. "I think some of the bulls the league uses might still come from their breeding, but that always depends anyway. You said he got hurt?"

"He mentioned a shoulder injury. Shoulder and elbow."

"Ah yeah, that's shit luck. Bullriding wrecks you, if it don't kill you."

"Well thank heavens he escaped that," I say. It has been less than three hours, and already I have thought more about rodeos than ever before in my entire life. Their danger had never occurred to me.

"You're bored already, aren't you?" Bits asks, as Dolly takes the popcorn back.

"I am not!" I protest. "Perhaps *rodeo* things aren't going to be my interest, but the society that we'll be briefly dipping into is new and interesting."

"Oh yeah! You'll get to rub elbows with both rodeo people and ostrich barons!" I suppose I should be pleased that Bits is somewhat indifferent, and Dolly is this enthusiastic, but Dolly's enthusiasm can be a chaotic ingredient. All in all, though, it is better than them preferring not to take the job at all.

"Well that's settled then," I say. "I'll call him in the morning and get all of our particulars ironed out."

"Sounds good," Dolly says. She offers me the bowl of popcorn, and I look at it for a moment, then lean over and take a handful.

"Thank you."

Chapter Three

I wasn't even aware that we knew somebody who tailored dragonscale here, but in the morning, Bits and Dolly are leaving without me peculiarly early, perhaps hoping to escape my scrutiny.

"We know how to dress ourselves," Dolly says and I very pointedly look her up and down. Ripped jeans, what I'm certain is a man's white undershirt, black bra, the same boots she always wears, and a canvas jacket over it that might be surplus and might actually be fashion, it's just that close sometimes. Bits snickers, and I look at her cargo pants and t-shirts, because she's wearing a long sleeved shirt under a short sleeved one. "We aren't *naked*," Dolly says, as though the two statements are equivalent.

"Can I at least send you with specifications, if you'd prefer to escape my watchful eye?" I sigh. I do dearly want to attend a suit fitting for these two, but there are other things on my to do list.

"Yes, give us some examples," Bits says, and waits for me to text her. "It's a more solid cover if we're to Bristol's specs," she says, and Dolly rolls her eyes elaborately, but she's smiling.

"Sure, sure. Today it's suits, you just wait and see what she does to us next time, now that she's got her foot in the door." Dolly's still going as Bits pushes her out the door ahead of her.

Once they're gone, I do a little bit of light searching on society pages, and gossip streams that I favor, to see what they say about Rafe and his family. To see how ostrich-y I can expect the property to be, and thus inform my clothing decisions. He and his brother have really been *very* rodeo focused for a number of years, and yes, his brother does run around a little and Rafe has not, that I can see. His brother's looks are flashier, but both of them are very handsome gentlemen. What a distinctly odd situation this is; was there ever a time I just wanted a rich, handsome man to take me away from all this? Perhaps years and years ago, when I'd just started out.

I call Rafe, and he answers hastily, eagerly. "I was starting to think you'd reconsidered," he says, laughing in an effort to cover how serious he is.

"No, I am *quite* intrigued, and my colleagues have agreed that the job is a compelling one," I say.

"Didn't take much convincing, I hope?"

"One of them is evidently a fan," I say.

"Does that make this easier for you or harder? I'm still real embarrassed that I just walked up to you at a party and—" My goodness, I can imagine him rubbing the back of his neck, squinting a little, abashed. What striking luck our encounter was.

"No, it's a fantastic meet cute."

"A what?"

"The story that we'll tell of how we met. I caught your eye across the room at an otherwise unremarkable party, and we hit it off immediately. I told you about a cocktail you'd never had before, and you're tall, dark and handsome, just the way the fortune teller always said I would marry."

"The fortune teller?"

"Perhaps I'm getting a bit nostalgic. Though don't all fortune tellers always say that?"

"I've never been to a fortune teller." He sounds interested and a little baffled. The more he talks, the more I enjoy his voice, and have a sense of the clothing that I'm packing.

"Oh you *must*," I say.

"Well if you say so," he says, bemused. "Is that just a thing you can do online?"

"I'm certain you can, but I find it's best to do so in person." That seems like excellent tabloid fodder indeed. Washed-up bullrider and his mysterious fiancée consult mystic. "I'll see if there are any local that are of good enough reputation that we should consult them, or if we'd have to go elsewhere."

"Is there a ratings website for that? Like how they do for restaurants?" He sounds amused. He does seem like a very nice man, and I do hope that continues to be the case for our several weeks of association. Otherwise, it shall be such a chore.

"We may be getting away from the construction of our narrative." I hold up a dress to myself in the mirror, consider whether it's too city-suited. "Who is it that you'll need to convince most, that this engagement and marriage isn't a sham? A lawyer?"

"My Great-Aunt Gertrude. She's still the executor of the trust. Maybe executor isn't the right word, but you get the gist."

"I do indeed. And what is Great-Aunt Gertrude like? Is there anything that she absolutely can't abide?"

"I think she hates gardenias," he says, without much of a pause. "Honestly, she probably won't be a concern but..."

"I'm sure she just wants her dear nephew to be happy." I put the dress back in my closet. "I do think that I'm going to need to go shopping."

"The girls do that a lot, so you'll be right at home. Maybe it'll be a bonding experience for you."

"The girls?"

"Yeah in the neighborhood. Well, I guess you wouldn't call it a neighborhood, but it's the group of our houses closest together I guess, in the scheme of things. Some family, some friends. They're people we'll see a lot, so we need to fool them too." Does he sound just a little disheartened?

"Just for a little while," I remind him. "I shall do my utmost to make certain this goes smoothly."

He laughs a little. "I believe it."

"Now when shall our second date be? And where? Have you selected a ring yet?"

"A ring?"

"Yes, darling, an engagement ring. Do you want to do a public proposal, or shall I just be suddenly wearing it from one appearance to the next?"

"I confess I hadn't given it that much in-depth thought." I wait him out, selecting shoes. While I have a variety of boots, cowboy boots are not among them. Perhaps they have charms of which I was not aware? "There's a family ring," he says finally. "I can get that from the bank."

"Only if you're certain. I wouldn't want you bringing out an heirloom for a farce."

"Well it isn't doing anybody any good where it is." I do approve of that sentiment. Fancy and special things are to be appreciated, not locked away; otherwise they might as well not exist.

"I will take the utmost care with it, of course."

"I appreciate it. So your, uh, bodyguards were on board?"

"Yes, they're settling their attire as we speak."

"Fair enough. I'll make sure my staff knows to loop them in and everything."

"Perfect."

"Is it weird that I'm looking forward to this?"

"I wouldn't say so, no. I'm sure it will be very interesting, and perhaps at least a little bit fun."

"There'll be plenty of parties, I hope you're ready for that."

"It's as though I've been training for it," I say with a little laugh. He laughs with me, and I do hope that after our faux engagement and marriage ends, he ends up finding somebody to spend his time with. He seems like a very nice man indeed, and I'm rarely wrong in these things.

Bits and Dolly come back not long after, wearing their new suits, and also cheap plastic sunglasses they must have procured at a convenience store, and fedoras, which I have no earthly idea where they would have gotten or why. From the same person who did the suits, presumably. Bits' pants are perhaps slightly too long; I assume she intends to fix that with different shoes.

"It's dark and we're wearing sunglasses," Dolly says, grinning.

"Yes, you are," I say, mystified.

"Aw, come on Bristles, I thought you loved old movies."

"Why yes, I do, but I don't get this reference, darlings, I'm very sorry."

"It's fine," Dolly says, pulling her sunglasses off and tucking them into the suit coat pocket. "Do we pass muster, ma'am? What are we calling you?"

"I went with Madison this time," I say. "And yes, that is as close to what I envisioned as I can expect."

"Well that's a great endorsement," Bits says, opening a bag of snacks she produced from I know not where.

"You *did* say that—"

"*Any*way," Dolly says. "Do we have a move-in date? Do we need a vehicle for that? We should probably have something that's 'ours,' right?"

"I hadn't thought of that. Yes, I expect we must." There's always some vehicle or other Dolly procures for our operations, but whether it's appropriate for the sort of persona that I am putting forth varies wildly. Our current vehicle is not. "I leave that to you, of course."

"Of course," she says, grinning. "Don't you worry, Miss...what's Madison's last name? You haven't used her in awhile."

"You're correct, I haven't, which is why it makes sense to do so now. Calloway."

"Miss Calloway," Dolly says.

"And the two of you...?"

"Well we talked about that, and figured we'd keep it simple with Darlene and Beth."

"Simple enough," I say. "It seems like we've made some preparations, but probably not nearly enough. What are we forgetting?"

"I'm making you a panic button," Bits says.

"Pardon?"

"To add to your bracelets. So that if it isn't really possible for you to talk at the moment, you can hit it and we know to bail you out."

"Yeah, you can put it with your...actually you don't use a bracelet phone anymore, do you? I noticed but I didn't notice." Dolly cocks her head, a little perplexed.

"Those fell out of vogue," I say.

"Oh of course, what was I thinkin.'"

Bits sighs. "But anyway, that makes sense, right?"

"Yes, it absolutely does, thank you."

She finishes her chips, and then she and Dolly go out again, to car shop.

Chapter Four

I'm not entirely certain how much property Rafe's ostrich farm comprises; Bits could tell me, as without a doubt she's looked it up, but I prefer to discover it, or not, on my own. We come up the drive at the appropriate time, Dolly driving, Bits in the front with her. They came up with a sleek and subdued black sedan which may or may not have been some manner of auctioned law enforcement vehicle, or a seized vehicle auctioned by law enforcement. I'm not entirely certain of that either, other than the knowledge that those auctions are frequently cash, and I can just imagine Dolly's smug joy at walking through such a transaction and coming away with the now-legitimized merchandise.

Rafe is on the front steps of a tastefully rambling two-story affair, the original house of which was probably built quite a long time ago, and then added on to as the family required. I wonder if he's been hoping I wouldn't show up. Or was he pacing nervously in anticipation, pleased to be taking this step in acquiring his family's fortune, regardless of the subterfuge? I could ask, but it is more fun to guess for myself.

He opens the car door for me mere moments after Dolly has put it into park, and hands me out. I catch a glimpse of people in the doorway, but don't have the time to parse whether they're staff or family or friends, as he is on one knee in front of me and that requires my full attention.

"I'm sorry I didn't have this for you the other night," he says with a smile. He's rehearsed the line, but the smile is genuine, I think. While I haven't purposefully rehearsed being proposed to, this is certainly not my first one.

"Rafe, it's just beautiful," I say breathlessly, but audible to our audience. The ring slides perfectly onto my finger as though it were sized just for me, and I'll assess later if I think it's the heirloom one or not. Then he clasps my hands as he stands, and it's the right moment for it, so I lift my chin and he leans down to kiss me. So far as first kisses go, it is more than adequate.

When we separate, there is a smattering of applause from the audience, and they come down the stairs to us. "R.J. said you were just a doll," a brassy blonde woman about my age says, taking me by the arms and looking at my face. She's wearing quite a lot of jewelry. "We were all very surprised!"

"I imagine you were," I say. "I was a little surprised myself."

"You'll have to tell us *all* about it," she says in a conspiratorial tone, and then lets me go so the next woman can greet me, a shorter brunette.

"We thought for sure that R.J. would just be a bachelor for life," the brunette says.

"You haven't even let me introduce her," Rafe says, gently interposing. "Madison, this is Paisley, and this is Rosalie. Ladies, this is Madison."

"We're sorry, we were just very excited," Rosalie, the brunette, says. Paisley sort of makes a little mouth, her eyes gleaming, intent; I can see who runs the parties, unless I'm missing my guess. There's something else, though. Oh, this will be interesting.

"We're hardly overwhelming," Paisley says. The men hung back a little, but they come and shake hands now, Ned and Paul.

"Maybe I'm feeling protective," Rafe said, chuckling. "I didn't even have the whole crew over, just you."

"We feel very privileged." Paisley smiles up at him. Oh yes, there was something else. "He even let me organize lunch," she says to me.

"Did he indeed?" I glance over my shoulder at Bits and Dolly, standing by the car. "Would it be possible for you to tell my people where to park, and where to bring our bags?"

"Yeah, don't worry, Gerald's going to take care of them for you." I raise my eyebrows at Dolly, who nods. It's quite alright for us to separate, we've all got our tiny, cunning earbuds.

"Perfect, thank you."

"Shall we?" Paisley asks. She seems determined to get me away from my supposed fiancé and finally he lets her, going over to talk to Dolly for a moment as another man, presumably Gerald, appears. "We'll get a mimosa in your hand and show you around a little on the way to the brunch table."

"That does sound delightful," I say. Mimosas and brunch are certainly a route to my heart. The entryway is as expected, with a sweeping staircase to the second floor, and a large gilt mirror in the front hall. It is hard to resist a mirror like that, and I comfort myself by thinking I'll revisit it later, but then Paisley has my arm again and we clack over there in our heels; the floor is polished tile. Standing next to each other, we're of about the same height as well.

"We're like sisters," she says, beaming. "You'll fit right in with the family!"

"I think I need to learn everybody's connections," I say carefully, and she laughs. She doesn't exactly seem like a cousin.

"You will! We're just all so cozy here in the neighborhood, you'll figure out who's who in no time." She gives me a conspiratorial little smile, and I smile back.

"And you're here to help me, of course."

"Of course!" Just a split second too slow, but I think she's still trying to work out if she's going to like me or hate me. I think she had intended to hate me on sight and is perhaps surprised that isn't the case." We wives need to stick together!"

"That we do," I say. My earbud clicks then, Bits letting me know that everything is proceeding smoothly. I assume she's making sure the suite is suitable, both for comfort and privacy. I assume Dolly has already cowed and then befriended all the rest of security. We each have our strengths. Do I wish I was prowling the estate and familiarizing myself with its nooks and crannies? Getting a sense of the staff? Yes, I do. But I'm also wildly curious about this little neighborhood clique of very wealthy individuals.

"Let me admire the ring," Paisley demands, and she has my hand before I can offer it, but also lets it go with only cursory examination. "He's definitely serious, that's the Sutter ring alright."

"Did anything suggest he wasn't serious?" I ask innocently.

"He's never brought anybody home other than—" Rosalie is silenced with a cutting, eloquent glance. "Not since just after high school," she recovers.

"I see. We didn't discuss any of that, I'm afraid."

Paisley's eyes darken a little, but then she pulls up another smile. "Of course you wouldn't! Why waste time talking about past flings." She does seem to have forgotten the notion of a preliminary tour, though.

The others are already seated in a very nice and airy room, one wall of which is entirely glass, allowing the morning sun to flood in. I'd somewhat expected the furniture to be gaudy or tacky, or even careless and too utilitarian, whatever a former bull rider would have an assistant fill his house with, but the table, chairs, and sideboards are all very nice and understated wooden pieces, perhaps antiques. Maybe this was purchased six generations ago, before their ostrich barony days and when they only had cattle, and has been in this room ever since. That seems distinctly possible.

The guest couples are arranged at the sides of the tables, Paisley and Ned, Rosalie and Paul. Rafe is at one head and I am at the foot, as is proper. Of course, there's probably a finishing school or at least manners lessons that each one of these individuals had, in addition to a debut ball, I'm certain. Now that I have names, I can look. Or have Bits do it, but why should she have all the fun? She won't see the significance in the same details that I would.

"Shall we toast the happy couple?" Paisley says, nearly the moment that we're seated, picking up her flute of mimosa. Rafe looks a little uncomfortable; I'm certain he doesn't prefer the formality of this setting. Perhaps he's unused to lying in general, and more specifically, to this inner circle of his friends.

"Don't let's make a big deal out of this at every meal," I say with a little smile. "I'm sure there are other opportunities on the horizon!"

"You've got that right," Rosalie says, with a bigger laugh than I was expecting. "This is just the everyday bosom friends, you're going to be hip deep in Sutters pretty soon here."

"Will I?" I ask, and raise an eyebrow down the table at Rafe.

"Only because you aren't as tall as me," he says with an easy smile. "Some extended family, yes. Not a circus like Rosalie is saying. Great-Aunt Gertrude. My older cousins who don't brunch, but live down the road a piece."

"It all depends on what you call a circus, R.J., your lady love might have a different definition," Paisley says sweetly, and then we have crepes suzette in front of us and our mimosas are re-freshed, and the conversation becomes a bit less adversarial. By accident or design, the men are all at the one end of the table, and 'us wives' at the other, and we carefully navigate our getting to know you small talk and my earbud clicks again, a double-click.

//These're nice digs, Madison// Dolly says quietly. //Bitsy didn't find anything wrong with anything, and I can't either. I'll walk you through the exits once we're all reunited, but you can just relax right now I think. They're letting us hang around in the hallway outside and offered us coffee and everything.//

"Oh, splendid," I say to Dolly, but also to Paisley, who has just said that dinner will be at her house tomorrow evening, so I needn't worry about it at all. I hadn't been; this house has a staff, I'm certain I won't worry about dinner at all. My party planning prowess mightn't be called upon at all, more's the pity.

At the other end of the table, R.J. is talking about the rev-enue or return on ostriches or some such; the business side of it definitely sounds like he's still getting comfortable with the words in his mouth. The livestock handling aspects, though, he's clearly a natural at.

"Now I'm unclear, do you all ranch ostriches? Is that even the proper word to use?"

"We do, yes. All this land used to be Sutter land, and when they cut back on the cattle, on account of the ostriches, other families were able to move in and take part in the same types of concerns. It's just plain luck that we kids all got along so well, isn't it Paisley? Well maybe sometimes we all fought like cats and dogs, but that's part of growing up." Rosalie seems to be a creature without guile, and it is refreshing. I do think it means that I need to be all the more wary of Paisley's hidden claws.

"It certainly is, and I'm sure it makes you all that much closer now that you're adults."

"What about your family, Madison? Will we be meeting any of them?" Paisley asks.

"My family? I'm afraid I'm tragically orphaned," I say, sipping my mimosa. The panic button that Bits made me blends quite nicely with my other bracelets. I suppose some technology related skills extend to other disciplines. "It's just myself and my bodyguards, no more and no less."

"Your...bodyguards."

"Yes, we've worked together ever so long now, they're practically my sisters."

//Who share the profits// Bits mutters.

"But you don't have *any* family at all?" Rosalie asks, wide eyed. Her shock is very touching. I'm sure, were she to know the truth, that I walked away from a quite living family in order to make myself a better, if entirely fraudulent, life, she would be entirely beside herself.

"You're such a darling, don't be sad for me. I'm quite used to it."

"Does that mean your half of the church will just be your bodyguards?" Paisley asks, and Rosalie gapes at her.

"Paisley, you can't just ask somebody that."

"We're all family here," Paisley says, eyes glittering. "Or we're close enough now, isn't that right?"

"It means I won't have a side of the church," I say, and then pause, smiling sweetly. "Though perhaps we'll elope, and dispense of the need for such things"

Paisley laughs as though I've said something very foolish and impossible, and Rafe casts us a quizzical look from the conversation at the other end of the table. "Elope? Great-Aunt Gertrude would never stand for that!" She shakes her head. I maintain my smile, though.

"I suppose she'll just have to sit, then." There is just the *slightest* of pauses, and then Rafe laughs, and the rest of our guests follow suit.

Chapter Five

Our brunch guests stay for an interminable amount of time. They're Rafe's friends, so clearly he does not feel as though he is entertaining them; they've just always been there. They take me all over the house, and eventually, Dolly trails us at a near remove. I assume Bits has decided to remain in the suite and traipse about in the ranch's cyberspace. I'm certain Dolly wants to get a broader sense of the property, and of the staff. Perhaps also Rafe's friends, though I'm confident that I have Rosalie's measure. Paisley, I shall need a little more time with. From her attitude, though, it seems I'll have ample opportunity.

There is quite the expansive gym setup, but Rafe doesn't take us in there. I see Dolly craning her neck, presumably to catch a glimpse of the mechanical bull, if there is one. It's only the first day, we'll find out.

Rafe keeps my arm comfortably threaded through his, and matches my pace as we go. He looks at my shoes more than once, especially when we venture outside, but seems to have decided that if I don't say anything, he won't either. The other ladies are wearing lower heeled sandals. Well, the other *guests* are, Dolly is wearing some manner of combat boots. I don't need to even look to know that's true.

"R.J. who *is* that?" Paisley asks eventually, catching sight of Dolly at one point as she turns to say something to her husband.

Rafe glances, barely; he'd already noticed, clearly. "She's one of Madison's bodyguards," he says easily, as though this is a completely normal occurrence. I think, after our first meeting, I hadn't expected his complicity in his own scam to be quite so polished.

"*One* of Madison's bodyguards?" she asks, eyebrows and tone climbing.

"Come on, I keep telling you, don't screech around the ostriches," Rafe says, smiling, and he glances at me. The ostriches in question are not at the very picturesque fence, but rather further out in their field. I assume they don't care much for human companionship, they aren't pets.

"I wasn't screeching," she says petulantly, but with her tone adjusted. "Why does Madison need bodyguards? More than one bodyguard?"

"I guess she likes feeling secure. Why are we talking about Madison in front of her like she ain't here?"

"Oh don't say ain't," I say before I can stop myself. I'd given up correcting Dolly's periodic usage, I was not prepared for Rafe's. I smile apologetically, and he laughs.

"Yes, dear," he says, and pats me on the hand, very natural. I suspect perhaps he overstated his guileless nature. I catch Paisley's reaction just barely, from the corner of my eye; I wonder when they were an item, and for how long. And what Ned thinks of their history. Maybe he thinks Rafe was a fool to lose her.

I wonder if she one day thought that the Sutter ring would again be hers.

The ostriches remain disinterested in us, despite Paisley's screeching, to my relief. I am more than a little surprised at just how large they are. I knew, of course, but had never seen them even this close previously. I don't find birds particularly engaging; to me, they lack the cuteness that a puppy or kitten does. I suppose I am in general simply not an animal person, as Dolly was more than happy to prove to me during our Macau adventure.

By the time our guests finally get into cars and depart to their respective neighboring homes, Rafe seems to have settled very comfortably into the deception. He isn't too demonstrative, but just enough. Thoughtfully so, without being too touchy. We wave from the front steps as though we're doing the end-credits scene for our very own reality show, and then he sighs, loosens his collar, and turns to Dolly.

"Nice to meet you..." he says, extending a hand.

"Darlene," she says, and gives him a firm enough grip that he's surprised. "The other one's Elizabeth, not sure how often you'll see her."

"Fair enough," he says. "Do you do this kind of thing often?"

"Not really," she says with a grin and a shrug.

"Our jobs together have varied," I say.

"Fair enough," he says again. "That went okay, right?"

"I think it went very well indeed."

"Good, good." Now that we're all here, he doesn't seem to know what to do about that, exactly.

"Do we have a schedule of upcoming get-togethers, so that I know when they are and how to dress for them?"

"I think Paisley sent me a thing, yeah."

"She always arranges your parties, then?" Dolly grins but clearly keeps from laughing.

"Yeah, she's great like that." He looks up at me from his phone. "Oh, though I guess you would normally be taking that over, wouldn't you."

"Normally, yes. Given our plan, though..." Rafe sends the information to my phone, and I scroll through brunches that are just me and the other women, a larger friends and family party, some dinners. He's paying us well and I do enjoy parties. Then a thought strikes me.

"Oh! I'll have to go wedding dress shopping."

This time Dolly *does* laugh, and Rafe slowly blinks. "I...I guess you will."

"Obviously, you won't be attending that. But I should invite Paisley and Rosalie, yes?" Or perhaps not, given the history...

"I'm sure they wouldn't want to be left out," he says slowly.

"And they can tell me where their wedding dresses came from, it's a perfect bonding opportunity."

"I didn't think you'd be so eager to—"

"Nonsense, it's certainly under the umbrella of what we discussed. I can't spend all my time by the pool, I have my complexion to worry about."

"Right."

"Just let me know if there are any topics I should avoid? Or areas of the house?"

"Nothing I can think of." That's a relief; I didn't expect him to be a Bluebeard, especially not with a former bride visiting at will, but boundaries are important.

"Okay, good. I'll text them about it this evening. Is there anything else you'd like me for today?"

"No, you more than earned your keep already." He makes a face, and suddenly seems all too aware that Dolly is standing nearby. "That feels like the wrong thing to say."

I laugh, and lay a hand on his arm. "It's all right, I know what you meant."

"I'm glad." He smiles and shrugs. "But no, you can do whatever. Use the pool, I know what you already said. Use the training room. Just be careful of the equipment, don't want you to hurt yourself."

"Oh, Darlene is well aware of the workings of mechanical bulls, from what I understand," I say airily, and he raises his eyebrows and looks at her.

"Are you really?"

"Just from a casual, drunk at the bar perspective, yeah," she says, laughing. "But also, I know who you and your brother are."

"And Madison didn't." He grins at me.

"I don't know who *any* sports figures are," I say. "I can't be expected to."

"I suppose not." His phone rings and he looks at the screen and looks at me. "Anyway, enjoy your day. You know how to get a hold of me, if you need me. And any of the staff can help you with meals or whatever you need."

"Thank you," I say, and step away so he feels comfortable taking his call.

"Well ain't he dreamy," Dolly says with a wicked grin, and we fall into step as she takes me to the suite.

"You knew that already," I say, perhaps more impatiently than I feel. He is a very handsome man. He seems kind, and unusually emotionally perceptive.

"More than you."

"To my advantage, n'est-ce pas? He isn't looking for just another...buckle bunny." What an awful, if illustrative, turn of phrase.

"Nah. It also means you'll probably feel bad if we lift anything from here. Family jewels, wherever those are. Antique guns from the Alamo. The golden spike from the transcontinental railroad."

"Oh, that's in a museum in the Bay Area," I say. "It's best if we don't 'lift' anything from this property, correct."

"*This* property," Dolly says. "So other places we visit..."

"Let's just be discreet, shall we? We're already getting a payday out of this situation. I'm certainly not *against* getting a bonus, but—"

"Readin' you loud and clear, boss," Dolly says.

Chapter Six

There was a time I would have confidently said that of course every girl has imagined her wedding dress, but then I met Bits and Dolly. Their wedding aspirations, or lack thereof, aside, I have certainly imagined *my* wedding dress. And I confess, I have had a running file for a number of years, containing designers and styles which have caught my fancy.

The issue with marriage in my particular line of work is I've been enjoying my freedom so thoroughly, I'm uncertain about stopping, and settling down, regardless of the nest egg I have built for myself, and the hotel in Morocco that still waits for me, run by efficient staff whom I pay handsomely. I've spent so little time there, even though it is truly a life's dream come true. Maybe somebody else would have stopped and settled down, but it seems so early to do so. There's so much *time* left.

Paisley has a shop in mind, with a seamstress and designer who she went with, and so Dolly and Bits drive me there to meet them that Tuesday afternoon. "You sure you don't want us to hang around?" Dolly asks.

"Quite sure. You can occupy yourselves nearby, and I'm certain your services and supervision wouldn't be needed anyway."

"Aw, you don't want my opinion on dresses? I'm really hurt, Bristles."

"I'm sure you are," I say, rolling my eyes.

"There's a surplus store down the street," Bits says. "And I'm honestly not sure what I'd bet on taking more time, you in a bridal shop or Dolly in a surplus store."

I laugh. "I'd say I'm insulted, but I'm not sure either."

Dolly shrugs. "Depends on what I'm lookin' for."

"Do you have something you're looking for?" Bits asks.

"No, but I can always look." Dolly grins at me in the rear view mirror, and Bits shrugs an eloquent 'see what I mean?'

"That works out perfectly," I say after a moment.

"Sure does. I didn't really want to hang out and watch you get loaded anyway."

"Pardon?"

"Don't they have champagne and stuff for these things?"

"I hadn't considered that, but yes, probably. I'm *highly* unlikely to 'get loaded.'" It is with effort that I don't make a little face at that.

"Maybe not you, individually. Collective you, the other rich girls." We pull into the parking lot; Paisley and Rosalie are standing out front waiting, Paisley in a wide-brimmed hat and large sunglasses, Rosalie smiling and bareheaded, waving when I got out of the car. Rosalie is very sweet; I can just imagine the two of them in high school, maybe as cheerleaders. Would the Sutter boys also have done something like football, or would they have concentrated on rodeos even then? It's so delicious and unusual for me to know so little about the main interest of a social group. "You have fun now," Dolly says, like a movie mom dropping her child off at the mall.

"I'm certain we'll do our best," I say.

"I'll be listening in if you need us," Bits says quietly. "And you have your panic button."

"I do and it will be *fine*." I close the car door, laughing a little. The idea of that sort of trouble at a bridal shop is simply absurd.

"I'm so surprised your bodyguards won't be lurking with us," Paisley says, managing to keep her smile just short of a smirk.

"You don't think we'll need them here, do you? I'd only just convinced them that it would be safe enough..." I trail off and make a show of turning to watch the car drive off.

Paisley laughs. "Honey, I don't think you'll need them at all, is my point."

"Oh, I see." They are just wild to know more, for me to explain, and I don't think that I will. "Let's hope not!"

Inside the shop is both airy and cozy at the same time, a cultivated intimate boutique experience. There are comfortable chairs and a low coffee table by a three-paneled mirror that one ascends a small dais to stand before, and little plates of single-bite hors d'oeuvres, along with presumably chilled cans of sparkling water and champagne. The woman who greets us is dressed so simply that her clothing probably cost more than the car that Dolly drove me here in, unless she is indeed the designer at this establishment.

"A Sutter bride, at long last!" she says, after air-kissing both Paisley and Rosalie. "It is my honor to do a showing for you today."

"I appreciate your hosting us at such short notice," I say.

"Oh the pleasure is mine." She extends both hands and takes mine. "Now let me look at you. I have examples of what previous Sutters wore, and some things in the shop which are a modernization of that aesthetic. Get yourself a drink, and let me take some measurements."

This isn't my first fitting, of course, though it is my first wedding dress fitting. It would be more poignant if it wasn't all fake, but it is great fun all the same. The other girls had their turn here, on the same little dais, in front of the same mirror. Though I do wonder if Paisley had *two* turns; I'm very, very certain that she and Rafe were previously an item, though I cannot say at this point what I think broke them up, nor why she would still be so chummy with him. Unless she is still holding out hope, that's very possible. Which makes her welcoming grace towards me quite a herculean feat; I almost wish that I could reassure her that I am not here to stay, but this is such a temporary arrangement, it's really unnecessary.

The dresses are lovely. They aren't couture, of course, but I wasn't expecting that. The canned champagne is a frugal choice, but there are many passable brands that package like that nowadays, and I'm not turning my nose up at it. The proprietress, Leah, who also designs and does some of the alterations herself, is very good; knowledgeable, but with her own vision, which I can respect. And she does indeed, in the smart mirror, show past Sutter brides, both early century and also back in the twentieth. She can put me in those dresses, and we have a great deal of fun preening in period dress, though I do notice Paisley getting tense about one or two of the designs.

"Won't you girls tell me what your dresses looked like?" I ask sweetly, stepping off the dais.

"I thought you'd never ask!" Rosalie says, popping up off the couch. We're all a little pink from the champagne, I think. "I got it here, of course."

Leah pulls up the image in the mirror. "Her church look was this, with the veil, and the overskirt." She taps the screen. "And then for the reception, both of those came off, and she had this mermaid tail skirt." A couple of more taps and Rosalie, in the mirror, has her hair and makeup done, and is adorned with jewels.

"How delightful!" I say, clasping my hands. "And you were radiant."

"Aw, thank you." She smiles, open and happy. "Paisley, you show her!"

Paisley is a little more reticent, but she takes her place. For a wicked moment, I'd like Bits to be listening in and working her magic, so that I know what the dress Paisley picked for her wedding to Rafe looked like. But I do not ask, and that does not happen. Paisley's dress is the sort of subtle that makes it flashy, in addition to a train that drips off the dais and stretches partway across the room.

"The train came off for the reception," she says, eyeing herself critically. "So it went from peacock length to just floor length." Leah shows us, and I'm sure to match my delight to what I showed Rosalie.

"It's perfect, it suited you so well! I hadn't considered that many add-ons and takeaways, I do love the tea length gowns so much." The less hampering of my movement the better, but those *trains*... "Perhaps an extravagant veil, to make up for it?" I ask, turning to Leah.

"We do have many options, even with your short turn-around."

"You're an angel," I say, and Paisley cracks open another can of champagne.

"So you decided, then?" she asks.

"Yes, this tea length one with the lace detailing," I say. "I have just the necklace to wear with that neckline."

"Is that your something old?" Rosalie asks. "Ooh, we need to get all that figured for you. What should you borrow? A purse? And what's *blue*?"

"I thought blue shoes might be delightful," I say. "I hadn't given a thought to the rest of it." That isn't entirely true, but I do want to see what they'll say.

"Your something old has to be the Sutter jewelry," Paisley says. "It's tradition. R.J. has it in a vault at the bank. And you'll borrow something from one of us, of course."

"You have just been so welcoming, I can never thank you enough." At the bank, that would make sense. I wonder when last anybody wore that jewelry. Did Paisley get to try it on? I will have to have Bits gather up the information on that for me, I simply won't have any time to do the sorts of society pages searches I might otherwise delight in carrying out.

"It's how we are," Paisley says, and her smile is *just* warm enough. "I'll have you over to look at my things this week." She pauses. "Tomorrow maybe? My, things are moving fast aren't they?"

"Well I could..." Rosalie starts shyly, but she stops before Paisley can cut her off.

"That's sweet, honey, but I think we're closer for hair and complexion."

"You're right," Rosalie says, with a doubtful little quirk of the lips that I'm not certain Paisley catches.

"Oh I'm sure I can borrow something from each of you," I say. It's wicked of me to disrupt their dynamic, I won't be here forever to maintain any changes that I effect, but I simply cannot help myself. But Rosalie brightens.

"You could! One of the parties is at my place the day *after* tomorrow, you could look then."

"See? Perfect." I smile, and Paisley finishes her champagne.

Chapter Seven

Bits fills me in when she and Dolly pick me up. "Paisley and R.J. were high school sweethearts, and she even travelled the rodeo circuit with him for awhile? He proposed to her from the ring after some award winning ride and—"

"Oh, now that you say that, I remember watchin' that livestream," Dolly says. "They put her on the jumbotron and everything, and then brought her down bawling into the ring."

"Had he planned it, or was it the euphoria of a...seventeen second bullride?" I cannot for the life of me remember the span of time they consider significant, just that there is a span of time that they consider significant.

"He had a ring in his pocket, so it had to be planned," Dolly says, then glances at Bits. "Sorry to interrupt."

"It's okay. I don't really know what broke them up, though. They were doing this long engagement with parties thing, your society type columns are really great for getting that information, and then just one day a week before the wedding, the whole thing was called off. He still paid the caterers and everything, but there was no wedding, no party, and then he went away for the next rodeo circuit and she stayed here."

"And then when did she marry Ned?"

"They announced their engagement that year and got married the next."

"That's kinda weird isn't it?" Dolly says.

"It is indeed." There is an obvious answer, of course, but it would have been mentioned by now, I would think. "She wasn't—"

Bits shakes her head. "Nope, no baby. No indication anywhere that she cheated or he cheated or anything. General speculation is she didn't want to be a rodeo wife, and R.J. wasn't willing to give up the rodeo life."

"I can understand not wanting to be a rodeo wife," I say. "What business is Ned in?"

"He's an accountant. It looks like he runs the books for his family's properties, which are some animals, some feed. They've got a patent on some kind of newer corn."

"New corn, Christ Jesus," Dolly says, and pulls out her ecigarette. We drive in silence for a few moments.

"So an accountant's wife, a bit more stable, a bit less glamorous."

"Boring as hell, I'd think," Dolly says. "Your accountant husband's life is exciting, you got the wrong kind of accountant." She exhales sugar cookie-smelling vapor.

"Or the right kind, if you're bored," Bits says.

"And is Paisley bored?" I get a text notification and pull it up. It's Rafe.

//We're invited out for dinner tonight with some shareholders. I said yes, but you don't have to come.//

"Her husband's boring and she's bored. She mostly just buys things and bullies her housekeeping staff, though. And plans parties."

//It's perfectly fine, I'll freshen up and be ready when you need me// I text back. //Where are we going?//

"What does Paisley like buying?" I ask. Bits blinks at me.

"Paisley has a couple of different things she collects. A certain pattern of china that was discontinued thirty years ago, glass figurines from an Italian company, and watches."

"Watches? Wristwatches?" I'd noticed Paisley wearing a watch, but it didn't seem particularly distinct. Or nicer than mine, which is a trinket-y little darling that I picked up in Johannesburg last winter. It hasn't got a single smart piece in it, it is purely mechanical, and it's certainly made me think that perhaps I might want to start a mechanical watch collection. When I actually retire for good and simply relax into a life of leisure.

"Yeah, wristwatches. She collects smartwatches, from vintage to modern. Different styles and functionalities, and even OSes. It's a little weird."

"If *you* think it's weird..." Dolly says.

"Well if she was into coding or VR or anything it wouldn't be weird, but she doesn't seem to be. Their house doesn't have any kind of equipment that reads like that, and while she's an always online kind of person, it's the social media type, not the swimming in code type. She livestreams making lemonade."

"Lemonade livestream," I say.

"Yeah, she's got one of those granite countertop kitchens," Bits says. "Gray and white and chrome everything else."

"Oh, *that* type." Dolly catches my eye in the rear view. "You know the type, Bristles."

"I'm certain I do," I say. "But I'm very interested in what you think about that type."

"Oh, you know," she shrugs. "There's just a certain kind of white lady that's like that." Bits is nodding and I can't help but laugh.

"Yes, I do know," I say. "Oh, Rafe says that we're invited out to dinner someplace tonight, so I suppose you two can lurk at your leisure, or remain—"

"At the ranch?" Dolly asks, and I sigh somewhat.

"Yes, at the ranch. At least it doesn't really *smell* like a ranch."

"Do you know what a ranch smells like?" Bits asks.

"While this is my first proper ranch experience, I assure you, I have seen animals before in my life."

"Sure you have," Dolly says, eyebrows climbing.

THE SHAREHOLDERS ARE dreadfully boring and ridiculously rich. After the introductory niceties, they in general talk business in a way that does not require my input, and Bits is a great help in keeping me occupied, by continuing to research the Paisley-Rafe romance that failed, and reading occasional items of commentary into my ear. Winning prizes for her at the little county fair, going to an exclusive club at the nearest big city, her being seen on shopping sprees, her at the hospital after each of his injuries. Maybe that was the reason why; she just couldn't stand seeing him hurt over and over, and not knowing if he would recover each time.

At one point, once we've finally reached coffee and cigars, some of the men are talking to each other and Rafe leans over, squeezes my hand, and says in my ear "I'm sorry this is so boring, I'll make it up to you."

I smile at him, a little startled. It's the perfect time for him to steal a kiss, and he does.

"We shouldn't be taking time away from the lovebirds," one of the men says. No check has come, and I'm not certain who arranged this or how, but there is a flurry of handshakes all around and that is that. One of them palms some folded bills into my hand and gives me a wink, and I wink back just slightly, smiling, and slip the money away without looking at it. Perhaps it isn't real money after all, but rather religious tracts; I've seen that more than once, what a dreadful trick people play on waitresses and the like.

"I hope that wasn't so bad," Rafe says, holding the car door for me.

"No, it wasn't so bad at all," I say, smiling. "And well within the scope of our agreement."

"I think you're lying, but it's hard to tell." He starts the car. "Well, let me show you something. Maybe it'll make things up a little."

"Rafe, honestly, there isn't anything to make up," I say, but he doesn't turn back towards the ranch.

//You okay, Bristol?// Dolly asks. I don't know if she's actually stayed at the ranch this evening, or if she followed me at some remove.

//I do think so, yes// I say.

//Well okay, just say the word if you're not.// I have never, in fact, had to say the word. It is a comfort knowing it's there, though.

We start to pass signs for historic attractions, and Rafe's surprise is ruined directly when I say "A carousel?"

"It's more than a hundred years old," he says. "Not originally from here, but moved here from someplace else and restored. And then it's weathered a bunch of storms. It's not normally open this late but, I know a guy." He gives me a sidelong glance and smiles.

We make a final turn, and then there it is, golden and lovely under the starlight. It begins its rotation as we get out of the car, the calliope playing merrily. I think there's a river nearby, or perhaps a lake, though I can't see it for the dark, just feel the breeze off the water. "It's beautiful," I say.

"I hoped you'd think that. You want to go for a spin?"

"Of course."

There is an attendant in the little booth, and Rafe stops and has a quiet word with him. I'm a bit surprised that it isn't automated, but I suppose an antique wouldn't be. I'm not certain many people are making modern carousels, what a shame. Bits would know.

The carousel slows, and we step up to select our animals. I have a moment of delicate indecision, next to a white rabbit with flowering wreaths serving as its saddle and bridle, and consider my dress. "Perhaps I ought to simply choose one of the benches," I say, indicating one which looks like a Roman chariot.

He laughs, then steps close. "Just ride sidesaddle," he says and, looking into my eyes, lifts me by the waist, as though performing a dance move, and sets me up on the rabbit in a way which allows me to modestly arrange my skirt.

"Why, you clever man," I say, and with the ease of ten thousand rodeos, he swings up onto the creature next to me, a beautifully rendered griffon.

The carousel picks up speed, the world beyond it smearing into a band of bright lights. I feel as though I ought to know the carousel melody, as it seems all carousels share the same one, but I can't place it even as it grows in volume, making conversation impossible. I wonder if Rafe ever brought Paisley to the after-hours carousel, and if this is a standard means by which he charms women. He is indeed *very* charming, which makes me wonder a bit at the necessity for our arrangement after all. But a deadline is a deadline, and once we've done our work, he'll be free to pursue a genuine romance.

The carousel slows again, the music growing gradually quieter, and Rafe helps me down again, still smiling. I lean on his arm when we step to the ground, delightfully dizzy. "Oh darling thank you ever so much, it's been ages since I've done that," I say, enchanted despite our arrangement.

"You're welcome," he says, and we pause in the golden puddle of light cast by a street lamp and he kisses me briefly, gently. When we step apart, I can feel myself flushing, just a little. "I hope that was okay to do." He sounds as though he isn't used to being confused on this point, despite having kissed me twice prior. It's within our arrangement.

"It was the perfect thing to do," I say, but as he leans in again, his phone rings, breaking the enchantment. He sighs as he pulls back, steps away to answer it. I turn to look back at the carousel, maybe see if I can spot lights reflecting off the water I think is nearby. It wasn't quite so cool at the restaurant, but here, the breeze raises goosebumps on my arms.

"Sorry about that," he says, coming back. "It's hatching season."

"Is everything all right?"

"Yeah, I was just ignoring their texts, so they wanted to be sure I was okay, and that I knew. It's my first real one, as it were." He looks at me, shrugs out of his jacket and puts it around my shoulders. "Here, I shouldn't have kept you out here like this."

"Oh, thank you." Hatching season; I've never given a moment's thought to the life cycle of the ostrich. Certainly I've never seen a baby ostrich in any of those posts of cute baby animals.

"Thank you, for being so patient with all of this. It's kind of embarrassing."

"Luckily for you, I very much enjoy parties."

"I sensed that about you, when I first saw you across the room."

"You didn't, but it's nice of you to say so." We walk back to the car, and the carousel lights stay on until we drive away. "Do you show that off to all of your dates?" I ask.

"You're the first," he says, and this time, I do think he's telling the truth.

BACK IN THE SUITE, Dolly is sprawled fully dressed on the still-made bed like she's been there the whole time, her boots hanging off the edge. So maybe she wasn't at a sniper's vantage the entire time I was out. I don't know what she was watching on the television, as she turns it off the moment I walk in.

Bits is reclined on a chaise longue in the corner, her VR headset pulled down.

"You clever man," Dolly says with a grin, and I laugh.

"There isn't any harm in stroking his ego," I say.

"No, I guess not," she says. "Plus you got a jacket out of it." When Rafe dropped me off at the entryway, I *did* try to return the jacket and he demurred, so I'm still just wearing it around my shoulders.

"I did, what do you think?" I do a little spin.

"Brings the whole outfit together," she says, but I'm not certain she's even looking.

"What did you buy at the surplus store? I'm so sorry that I didn't ask before dinner, but I didn't have the time."

"Oh, the usual sorts of things. A new ghillie suit, for the local flora. Boot laces."

"Is that all?" I take off Rafe's jacket and put it on the chair nearest the door, slip off my heels. What a full day it's been.

"Bitsy got some vintage binoculars, I didn't really follow why they're special. Some kind of smart but not smart tech? Oh and they had a display of stuff *for the ladies*, so I got you one of those pepper sprays that looks like a perfume."

"Goodness, you didn't have to do that. Thank you." Upon examination, it is a *very* tacky spray bottle, but that adds to the fun of it. It also makes absolutely sure that I wouldn't mistake it for one of my actual perfumes, were I reaching into a purse or pocket for it.

"Seemed like your kind of thing." Dolly swings off the bed and stretches. "Okay if we go off duty for the night, ma'am?"

"Of course, your time is your own. Honestly, you're taking this bodyguard thing far more seriously than I thought we discussed."

"Just keepin' up appearances," Dolly says, and kicks Bits' chair leg.

"I'm not asleep," Bits says.

"Didn't say you were."

"You could've said you were going to bed."

"I could've, but am I?"

"Are you?" Bits pushes up her headset and blinks up at Dolly, and then over at me.

"I am," I say. "I'm simply exhausted."

"There see, let's clear out so Bristles can do her rituals."

"You make it sound like witchcraft, I'm just washing my face and toning and moisturizing."

"Rituals." Dolly shrugs, grinning. "Anyway I'm gonna go play poker with some of the guys on staff, but you know how to get a hold of me."

"It didn't take you long to settle in," I say.

"Never does." Dolly winks and goes out the door to the hall, and Bits gathers herself and trails into the adjoining bedroom.

Chapter Eight

Dolly brings me around to Paisley's the next morning, and leans whistling against the car as I am greeted and brought inside. "Where's your other one?" she asks, still perturbed that I have bodyguards, but wanting to know the details in spite of herself.

"She had some technical things to go over. I don't know all of the particulars." The house seems to be an older one, I don't know what vintage I would say necessarily, but has very elegant architecture, and high ceilings. When it is very hot, it probably remains fairly cool in here, even without the addition of central air.

"Isn't it a little weird, that you don't know?"

I give a little laugh. "Oh, heavens no! That's what I pay her for, so I don't have to keep track of the technical things."

//It's very artful, the way Bristol lies// Dolly says in my ear on the little groupchat we three nearly always share. //There's some truth in it, more often than not.//

//It isn't fair to bait her while she has to talk to a mark// Bits says.

//It's the best time to bait her.// But she desists.

"I guess that's fair," Paisley says, laughing with me, though she's a little mystified. She takes me to a cozy little craft room that contains many shelves of materials, a very nice desk on which to organize those crafts, or perhaps letter writing, as there is stationery there as well. Regular pens and fountain pens and sealing wax, of all things, and an engraved brass lighter. "Can I trust you to keep a secret?"

"Of course you can," I say, and of course that is a lie that perhaps does not contain any amount of truth. But she seems satisfied, and removes a frame from the wall that contains a mosaic of photographs of herself and Ned, perhaps on their honeymoon. A little chrome safe is set in the wall behind, with a spinning dial combination.

"I keep the good stuff in here," she says. "The things I don't wear all the time."

"Very smart."

She spins the knob this way and that, and I don't pay too much attention to it. It is a little shocking, how easily she is trusting me. There has to be a reason, either security she has that she won't think I'm aware of, or just that level of carelessness. Or perhaps she thinks me so harmless, a threat only in that I'm taking Rafe away from her. Perhaps I should be more on guard, lest she turn with a gun in her hand and simply shoot me dead.

But of course what she turns with is a little carved wooden box of assorted trinkets, and the glimpse I get of the safe behind her is mostly of small boxes, manila envelopes, and the glint of what might well be a tiny private gold store that so many people of a certain demographic maintain, 'just in case.'

"The Sutter jewelry is a necklace and earrings, so you could borrow one of these rings, or a bracelet, or I have these doodads for in your hair," she says, opening the lid and turning the blue velvet interior towards me.

The bracelets are not precisely to my taste, and also don't go with my current assortment, which of course includes my panic button. I'd resolved myself to be amenable to her suggestions, and am relieved that the hair 'doodads' are some rhinestone combs that seem very vintage in appearance, and are wearable under the veil but will go quite well with the reception look. "You're sure this will go with the Sutter set?" I ask, resting my fingertips on them. "I don't want to upstage them, or look as though I'm not taking them seriously enough."

"They're perfect with them," Paisley says, her voice and smile a little brittle at the edges. She swiftly turns to find a box for me to transport them in.

"Thank you again for all of this, the parties, and welcoming me so readily. I really didn't know what to expect when I came here," I say.

"I'll be you didn't, whisked off your feet like that by R.J.," Paisley says. I still can't see her face, quite, as she fiddles with tissue paper, but her tone is a bit recovered.

"It's very unlike me," I say. "To be swept up in that manner. And you and Rosalie have just been so wonderful in helping me acclimate..."

"You and your bodyguards," she says, handing me the hair combs in their neat little package.

"Oh please don't tease me about them," I say, making a very pleading face, and she laughs.

"Tease you? I would never..."

By the time I ask after Rosalie, we've moved to Paisley's screened-in porch to have some lemonade. Dolly talking about white ladies with granite countertops floats through my mind.

"I'm surprised Rosalie wasn't here this morning," I say, to avoid talking about lemonade.

"It must just seem to you like her and I are joined at the hip," Paisley says, smiling but not.

"I haven't had such a close friend in ever so long, I might have been the teensiest bit jealous," I say in a confessional tone, and watch the surprise flicker in her eyes. If she thinks so little of Rosalie, why does she keep her around? Proximity?

"Other than your bodyguards, which I am absolutely not bringing up to tease you."

"Absolutely not," I say, and we smile at each other and sip our lemonade.

"Miss Rosalie had a doctor's appointment this morning," Paisley says.

"Nothing serious, I hope?"

"Well it might be serious, but it isn't *bad*, if you know what I mean." I blink at her for a moment, as I don't know what she means.

//She's talkin' about *babies*, Bristol// Dolly says.

Oh, of course. "Oh, she must be excited! Hopeful, perhaps?"

"Hopeful, definitely." That hangs in the air between us, and I consider that Paisley's household seems childless. "We've all got our schedules for things like that, and she's felt like her clock was ticking."

"Well the best of luck to her then," I say. I wait a moment, and then ask "And you?"

"Ned and I haven't started trying yet. I couldn't imagine having a baby in my twenties, I still feel like a baby." She looks at me intently. "Have you and R.J. discussed it yet?"

"*Babies?*" I'm more than a little aghast, but then I rapidly consider that she must know what his designs on continuing the Sutter line are and are not, and I don't. However, his focus has shifted considerably in his new post-rodeo world, and I would guess that even if he was not previously amenable to children, he likely is now. "We aren't in a hurry, to be sure."

"As opposed to your wedding," she says, but I don't rise to the bait. She must know about the trust deadline, and after a moment she flashes a smile. "Was just checkin' to make sure I wasn't planning a baby shower already as well."

"You would be among the first to know," I say. I can't say why I think that little detail doesn't ring entirely true, but of course young married women talk about babies all the time. I'm a little embarrassed that I needed Dolly of all people to prompt me. "After all, you and Rosalie are the best friends I've made here."

"I'm so happy to hear you say that."

DOLLY AND I ARE PART of the way back to the Sutter ranch when Marquis calls me. "I *know* you aren't getting married to some rodeo man without inviting me," they say when I pick up.

"Oh darling, of course I'm not. Or I am, but it's strictly business."

"Bristol..."

"His family trust has a date by which he is to be wed, or else it disburses elsewhere. We met at an otherwise dreadfully boring party, and hashed out the details."

"Of course you did. Where are Bits and Dolly in all of this?"

"They're acting as my bodyguards," I say.

"Bodyguards? And you aren't inviting me? This is ridiculous. An awful insult, I will never forgive you."

"I promise you, it is not the sort of fun to which you are accustomed."

"She's tellin' the truth," Dolly says, raising her voice. "Lotta dumb parties, lotta driving around."

"Engagement parties, I'm sure. What does your dress look like?"

"I'll send you a picture. But darling, how did you find out?"

"You aren't keeping up with your magazines," they say, and when I send a pair of wedding dress pictures, one with the veil and one without, they send me a link to a gossip column about R.J. Sutter's mysterious bride.

"Oh how *sordid*," I say, a little bit delighted, a little bit scandalized. Of course they don't have a single good picture of my face, I'm very careful about that, between clothing and make-up. But of course Marquis would recognize me, we've been thick as thieves for years. "And you're right, I'm woefully behind in my reading. Is there anything else I need to catch up with?"

"Not that can't wait until after your nuptials." We both laugh. "Is the plan also a splashy divorce, then? You're getting a good paycheck out of this, I hope, for the girls' sake if not your own."

"Yes, we're getting paid handsomely for this, I promise you."

"Good, I'm glad. I'll let you get back to your cowboy glamor, then, and you must visit me and tell me all about it once you're done."

"Of course I will, darling."

There is another vehicle parked in the drive, that Dolly stops behind. "Huh," she says, but doesn't continue the thought, as Rafe and another man come out the front door as though they've anticipated me, or were just well timed.

"Madison, this is my brother," Rafe says.

"Gabriel, I've looked forward to meeting you," I say, and he pauses in the middle of shaking my hand, a pained look on his face.

"Oh hell, at least call me Gabe? I heard you're calling R.J. Rafe."

"I certainly am, I absolutely will not call my fiancé something like R.J. And noted, of course."

He smiles, and we finish shaking. "Well okay then." He glances at Rafe, who shrugs in a classic 'I told you so' manner. "I guess we don't have to worry about you keeping up." Even as he says that, though, his eyes drop to my high heels and he raises an eyebrow.

"No, I don't think you do," I say.

"Madison, I told Gabe the whole thing, you don't have to pretend around him."

"Pretend what, darling, that we're madly in love? But what if it's the truth?" I smile wickedly, and they both laugh.

"I didn't think R.J. had it in him, to be honest," Gabe says. "Especially not after what went down with Paisley."

"Gabe..."

"You didn't tell her? She's gonna get an ice pick in the back and have no idea why." Gabe turns to me, shaking his head.

"I know they used to be an item," I say. "I was unsure of the breakup, but given how friendly they still seem..." trailing off, hoping Gabe will pick up the thread, and he does, bless him.

"Oh yeah, they're still real chummy. But you watch your back around her, she's still carrying a torch, and she'd drop poor old Ned if R.J. would only say the word."

"She'll be able to continue carrying that torch, we already have my graceful exit planned. I'm not interfering with her in any way." I think of how avid she suddenly was, in the baby conversation. "Though I don't envy your continued handling of her."

"Paisley's Paisley," Rafe says with an uncomfortable shrug.

"Isn't that the truth," Gabe says. "Now I'm starved, are we having lunch or not?"

I KEEP WAITING FOR Great-Aunt Gertrude to become a concern, but she remains a bogeyman. She would have been to visit sooner, or we to visit her sooner, but she has had some minor medical complications arise, and so while Rafe still visits her, and Gabe does, they don't want to tax her by introducing a stranger. There is discussion whether she'll be able to make the wedding, but that remains up in the air.

Still, I have Bits research things about her, that I'm adequately informed should we suddenly meet. She is, or was, a member of the local chapter of the Daughters of the American

Revolution, and has been active both with her local church and also a number of both social and charity organizations. Quilting and soup kitchens and the like. Very community minded, is Great-Aunt Gertrude.

I do think that some of my interest is in maintaining the most flawless facade possible in our little charade, which has been some of the most active diversion that I have had in some time. I do also think that I am fascinated by this family, these blood related people who all have a certain genuine care and fondness for one another. Seeing the manner in which they operate is foreign to me, and different from how my own family functioned, before I left them. Perhaps if they had been more like this, I would have been less inclined to leave. But no, that environment was simply unbearable; we were not born into fortune, in the way the Sutters had been. They rather put me in mind of Dolly and her brothers, when we've had occasion to work with them, though Dolly and company were also not born into fortune. People are always the most interesting puzzle of them all.

Chapter Nine

I do have some very short unscheduled time on my own, which is not caught up in the whirlwind of extravagant wedding planning or Paisley's neighborhood social calendar, and on one of those afternoons, I have Dolly and Bits take me to the charming little downtown so that I might look into the possibility of getting cowboy boots. Part of the reason is just to get away on one of my favorite diversions, but also I know it will be a crowd pleaser, both amongst the locals and Dolly, should I trade out my footwear for something more environmentally appropriate.

She in fact can hardly believe it. "You're giving up the black velvet combat boots?" she asks.

"I am not. Different situations call for different footwear."

"Oh so you're tired of wearing high heels all day on an ostrich ranch."

"I didn't say that either. Dolly, honestly, you're ridiculous. I thought you'd be happy." Perhaps I'll get a blue pair, for the wedding. No, that's too ridiculous.

"I'm ecstatic, Bristles. I didn't dare dream that one day it would come to this. Did I, Bits?"

"Nope." Bits doesn't move from her position of recline in the back seat.

"Bits, I'm so sorry, are you dreadfully bored? Dolly is obviously in her element, but you..."

"Bristol, I don't need to be physically anyplace in particular to be in my element," she says. "But I appreciate you thinking of me. It's interesting, seeing the different levels of internet security the different households here are using, and whether it extends to their devices or not."

"I hadn't considered that." Bits indeed always has her own puzzles.

"And at Rosalie's house, all of her appliances are online, and the refrigerator orders certain things when they're running low, and the thermostat is linked up to some health app she has that's—"

"None of our business, Bits, though I do know digital privacy is one of those things," I say a bit hastily. Of course they already overheard the baby talk, but it doesn't mean we need to rehash it. "We haven't been to Rosalie's house, Bits, why would you—"

"She's one of the people you've spent the most time with here, and there keeps being suggestion that we'll be at her house eventually. Though keeping you away is just another one of the ways that Paisley is exerting what control she can over the situation."

"She's a real piece of work," Dolly says. "Princess gets-her-own-way."

I laugh a little. "Dolly, honestly."

"I don't trust her."

"Yes, darling, you've said." She gets out her ecigarette instead of arguing further. "Okay, you can drop me here. I'll let you know when I'm done."

"Whatever milady wants," Dolly says.

"Surely you don't want to come *shopping* with me."

"Don't call me Shirley." I frown at her and she grins. "No, you're right. I'll park and be nearby, though. Have fun. You gonna get ostrich boots to match the mister's?"

"I'll have to see what they have available," I say, closing the door behind me. It's something of a relief, to be standing alone for the moment. We three do not normally spend so much time in such close quarters, even though I've spent mornings by the pool and Bits can make herself nearly seem like furniture with very little effort.

I stop in a little touristy boutique first, simply for the sake of it. It's the sort of shop which could exist anywhere in the world, except by the register it also includes a little spinner of local postcards, and a small display of items from local artisans. In their display of synthetic silk scarves, I think I see a pattern that I recognize Paisley as having worn, and it is unkind of me to judge her for shopping locally, but I do, a tiny bit. It is tiresome to be fair all the time. Our days here are numbered, but I select some postcards to send Marquis; we share a fondness for receiving physical mail.

I step back outside and orient myself towards the boot shop, and then I hear a familiar voice from across the thoroughfare, and I freeze, not unlike when Bits had her difficulties some time back and did what, in her lingua franca, she called rebooting. I hear my old name and I reboot. What an odd feeling to have, so unexpected, just a span of moments with no thoughts, no words.

Then I recover and the world comes swimming back to me but by then it's too late to fade into the crowd and become somebody else, somebody that Lorraine doesn't recognize, who she hadn't ridden the train into the bright city center with, pooling our grubby dollars between us for a cover charge as I learned to wheedle our way past the bouncers, the velvet ropes, the lines of undesirables that we were so close to being, except for a certain je ne sais quoi that I finally cultivated, fully, and she fell short of and so when I left I shed her as part of that old life, old self, my outgrown chrysalis. And now she is here and she recognizes me and I have to take care of her or else quite a lot will be ruined. Bits hasn't said anything in my ear yet, nor Dolly, who I'm sure is watching this grisly tableau unfold, but I can hear the emptiness, the pause of their bated breaths. And they're certain to snicker about it later, those wicked girls.

"Stephanie? Oh my god we thought you were *dead*! And then *feds* came around looking for—" she's saying as we rapidly close the distance between her as if to embrace, me dipping my hand into my purse for the taser that I've carried off and on since Dolly got them for us in Macau, cutting off as my left arm goes around her shoulders and the taser in my right hand makes contact with her belly and she's out like a light, sagging against me, but now I can't just *leave her*, after what she's said. What feds? How did they track me back *home* after Bits spent all her due diligence erasing all of us. Oh drat. Oh darn.

"Dolly, darling, I do think we need to talk to her," I say quickly and quietly, holding my dear old friend up, as though we are conspiratorially whispering together and will part again soon with promises to call each other lately, to go out some-time, to have dinner.

To her credit, there is no laughter in her tone, just business. "Understood, be there in a sec."

I stagger Lorraine to a bench and get us both sat, careful not to drop any of her belongings. I never, ever thought that I would see her again, and am entirely unprepared for how I might feel about it. Luckily, now is not the time to feel anything, but rather to handle the situation which has arisen. Boots will have to wait another day, though. She isn't entirely unconscious, but she isn't actively awake either, and it's a relief when Dolly walks up, still smoking her ecigarette, grinning casually like we meant to meet here. She gives Lorraine a cursory check-over, feeling her pulse as we prepare to change locations, and doesn't seem outwardly perturbed by what she finds.

"You've just had a fainting spell, darling, but the car is just here," I say, just slightly too loudly, so that any passers-by who decide to take inopportune notice will have an explanation that allows them to return to their lives, satisfied that nothing sinister is happening.

"Okay," Lorraine mumbles, and I think of times she was drunk but I was not, and we got ourselves to the bus or train, and back to our shabby abodes. I *never* think about the past, or at least not that far past. Oh this is dreadful. We're of very similar height and build, and always were, and so it is surreal to see Dolly handle her so easily back to the car, giving the impression that Lorraine is helping far more than she is.

Bits, double-parked, is in the driver's seat, her VR headset hung around her neck, and I get into the front seat and Dolly slides into the back seat with Lorraine. "Where to?" she asks, pulling back into traffic once the doors are closed.

"Gimme a sec." Dolly opens Lorraine's purse, makes a face, hands it to me. I look inside, open the hidden zipper in the side, and pull out her wallet. I don't think her ID is a real one, but it does say her local address, and I show Bits.

"We're just taking her home?" she asks.

I arch a brow. "What else would you suggest?" She shrugs, and drives. Dolly is notably quiet in the back seat, as is Lorraine. When I glance back, Lorraine is belted in, her head lolled back against the headrest. "Is she okay?"

"Probably never been tased before," Dolly says, rather than saying she doesn't know.

"I'm certain that's true." I certainly had not, before my association with Dolly. Then I remember that I am the one who tased Lorraine and feel an unaccustomed pang of guilt.

Her apartment building is a predictable sort, square and tall and with dubious security measures at the front door that simply require us to wave her phone at them. She's still a bit stunned, but more able to walk, and by the time we're at her apartment door, she's able to take her purse and get out the keys, though not field the lock, and Dolly grabs her wrist and guides the key home into the lock, a solution I had not considered. Inside, Bits goes to the kitchen and I hear the tap run, and Dolly deposits Lorraine on a nubbly looking couch that I'm certain is made from recycled plastics and probably came with the lease.

Lorraine looks at me, and her eyes fill with tears, and I drop onto the couch next to her and catch up her hands. "I'm so sorry to hurt you like that, darling, I just had no idea what you were saying and couldn't—"

But she interrupts me. "I'm so glad you're okay. You were *gone*." Two tears break free, tracking down her cheeks and dripping onto the couch between us, and I'm so startled that I tear up as well, dropping her hands in surprise. I am entirely unprepared to have any sort of feelings about deciding to leave my old life; what's done is done. But Lorraine is here, and if I've ever had the slightest semblance of regret, it was leaving her in the gutter that I climbed out of.

"I'm so sorry," I say again, and not for the taser this time.

"You wanna clue the rest of us in?" Dolly asks.

I take a brief moment to compose myself. "This is my very dear friend Lorraine. We grew up together." Dolly and Bits both have similar expressions of wide-eyed shock on their faces. "We used to dress up and go to clubs together, when we were old enough." I pause, and amend "*nearly* old enough, we had fake IDs of course."

"Even without the IDs, Stephanie could get us into almost anywhere," Lorraine says. Bits hands her the water, and she takes it, drinking automatically. "Clubs that actual rich people went to. We saw celebrities, sometimes. She just had that face. Has that face. You look *great*."

"Thank you," I say. "Honestly, darling, so do you." People used to mistake us for sisters; we didn't always correct them. Oh, this is dizzying. "What are you doing here? And what do you mean, people came looking for me?"

"Well, I figured if I was going to be poor and have a shitty job, I could do that anywhere. So I came someplace different. Plus the rodeos are fun." She drinks some more water, looks at Bits and Dolly. "You really knocked me for a loop, I didn't really see your friends. Like, I know all of you helped me get here but..." she trails off.

"This is Bits and Dolly," I say after the slightest hesitation. "I work with them."

"You work with them? What do you do?"

"Acquisitions," Dolly says, smiling easily, but I see her taking in possible exits, I'm not certain what else. Which piece of furniture to barricade behind in case of gunplay? How to most quickly and quietly incapacitate Lorraine if this should take a turn. A further turn. "Though right now we've been relaxing with some rodeo folks."

"That sounds nice," Lorraine says, sounding a little unsure.

"It can be," I say. "But what were you saying about people looking for me? Feds?"

"Well, they didn't really say who they were, but they seemed like feds. Shiny shoes. They had a few pictures, not many, and they said they were looking into you as a missing person. Which was really funny, because we were the ones you were missing from first." She laughs a little, drinks some more water. She seems more alert now, more normal. "Kind of a younger guy, blondish hair. A woman and another person, those two didn't say anything though."

"I can't imagine they learned anything useful."

"They didn't, they were really frustrated about it. I still have the guy's card, though." She looks around for her purse, and Dolly picks it up from the coffee table and gives it to her. She rummages for a moment, comes up with one of those little metallic business card holders, and I can't help but smile. She gets enough business cards, or intends to, to keep a holder like that. "Here."

It's plain white, good thick matte cardstock, and says Will Scarlet, of course. I wonder who his companions were, and if we met them in the course of the diamonds debacle, or if they're from elsewhere in whatever agency it is he works for.

There's a phone number, and an email address, and that's all. I pass it to Bits, who looks at it a moment, and then hands it back before pulling out her phone.

"Don't *call* him," Lorraine almost squeals, and Bits blinks at her, surprised.

"I'm not. I'm tracking him."

My phone pings, with a message from Rafe. //Sorry to cut into things, but Great-Aunt Gertrude is going to make an appearance tonight. Real brief after dinner, when we're doing the cocktails by the pool thing.//

//That's quite all right, thank you for letting me know.// I reply, then look at Lorraine. "Darling, we're going to have to go. Here, I'll take your number, now you have mine. This rodeo stuff is very intricate, but is only for the next week or so. We'll be able to catch up after that, does that sound agreeable?"

"How do I know you won't just disappear again?" she asks, a dig that surprises me a little, but is more than fair.

"I suppose you'll just have to take my word for it," I say. "I have no way to make it up to you, or assure you in such a manner that you'll believe me, but I also can't take you with me."

"I didn't ask you to take me with you," she says. The unspoken 'this time' hangs between us. This, and I have to go meet Great-Aunt Gertrude. I'll have time to compose myself.

I hug her, surprising both of us I think. "I will call you," I say firmly, standing up. "Do you feel okay? Do you need anything before we go?"

"No, I think I've recovered from my electrocution," she says dryly, and Dolly laughs, then stops herself.

"This one's pretty okay," she says. "Not stuck up like your other friends."

"Well thanks." Lorraine smiles crookedly, and follows us to the door to close it behind us. "Talk to you soon. Maybe."

"I promise," I say, and she closes the door. It latches a moment later.

We ride the elevator to the lobby in silence. And then go out to the car, Dolly in the driver's seat, Bits in the passenger seat, headset on already, hot on Will's electronic trail, I presume. I just know Dolly is going to— "*Stephanie?*"

"You can *imagine* why I might have changed it. So dull. Though none of us go by our real names, after all."

"Oh, I do."

"You cannot *begin* to convince me that your given name is Dolly."

"Oh it ain't, it's short for Haunted Dollhouse."

"It is *not.*" I was so foolish, not even five minutes ago, thinking I would have time to compose myself. Or she's doing this on purpose, as a distraction.

"Wanna bet?" She's grinning at me in the rear view.

"I am not *betting* you..."

"Not a big bet. Just a dollar. A thousand dollars? For fun."

"Please pay attention to the road." I sigh and try to look to Bits in appeal, but she's still in her headset and oblivious to our nonsense, accidentally or on purpose. "And how are we to know the final answer? Do you carry your birth certificate, that I'm to assume is undoctored?"

"Nah, you can call Butler."

It is with great effort that I keep from rolling my eyes. "He's sure to back up any ridiculous story you tell."

"If *you* call him, he won't know I'm involved."

"You are entirely impossible. And of course he will, why else would I call him?"

"Aw, it'd hurt his feelings to hear that, but suit yourself."

"He carries that torch for *you*, Dolly, he never gave me a second glance."

"Yeah, maybe." But she lets it go, for the moment, and I'm relieved. Dolly can be exasperating, but normally, there is only so much that her banter and teasing gets to me. This has not been a normal day.

Chapter Ten

Paisley is already at the ranch and whisks me away the second I set foot out of the car. "Did you hear that Great-Aunt Gertrude is coming for like, five minutes?" she asks.

"Yes, Rafe messaged me. You're so sweet for coming to help set up, but he said her arrival would be after dinner?"

"Yes, exactly, so I've made it so you don't have to worry about dinner at all. But we need to get you dressed."

"Thank you," I say, a little mystified. I haven't yet worried the slightest bit about dinner. "Does she have a particular cocktail she likes? Oh, I'm so thoughtless, is she even able to drink?"

"If she was, you'd never be able to separate Great-Aunt Gertrude from what she wanted, but no, she'll just want a lemonade. I brought that too."

"Paisley, you're a godsend." There is no earthly reason she should not want me to fail spectacularly to gain Great-Aunt Gertrude's approval, and yet, here we are. Maybe she failed to garner that approval herself.

"Aw, you're sweet," she says. In the suite, I allow her to throw my closet open and examine what I've brought. "You have such a lovely complexion for this shade of pink," she says, pulling out one of my favorite dresses which is just dressy enough for a party and just casual enough for broader wear. "Definitely wear this one."

"I think I'll step in the bathroom and freshen up a little," I say, waylaid by a memory of having similar conversations with Lorraine before a night out. I am not one given to nostalgia, this really must stop.

"I'll leave you to it, then. Just call me when you need me." And she flits off again.

By the time Bits comes to the suite, I've changed, washed my face, and applied a new face of makeup. "So that was weird," she says.

"I'm afraid you'll have to be more specific."

"Mostly the Lorraine thing." I look at her in the mirror as I put my earrings in. "What are the chances, right?"

"Astronomically low, one would have thought. And yet."

"And yet." She hesitates a second, chewing her bottom lip. "Are you okay?"

"Yes, thank you." There was a time in our association when things didn't get so emotionally messy all the time. "Were you able to find anything about Will? That wasn't the same number he used back when—"

"No, it was a different number, but I—"

"You're still in here?" Paisley bursts in. She's a little surprised to see Bits in the room and pauses a moment, but when Bits doesn't say anything, she comes to the dressing table. "Aren't you done yet?"

"Honestly, darling, I'm shocked to hear such a thing coming from you..." I say, standing up. "We girls have to stick together with regards to preparation times."

"It's true, we do, but sometimes prep needs to be the short version. You look ready, though, are you ready?"

"Yes, I'm ready." Perhaps Rafe sent her. Bits shrugs a little, barely noticeable other than to the discerning eye, so whatever she was saying must not have been terribly crucial. I allow Paisley to whisk me away to a fairly normal dinner, with herself and Ned, Rosalie and her Paul, and Rafe and Gabe. The seating arrangement isn't the usual; Gabe is seated next to me, not Rosalie, though she keeps shooting me agonized little glances when Paisley has her attention elsewhere.

Finally, when dessert is cleared and we're getting up to go to the verandah and greet the soon to be arriving guests for the cocktail party portion of the evening, Rosalie catches my arm. "Your dress," she says, getting a little jumbled in her haste, I think.

"Yes? Paisley helped me pick it out for this evening." I smile; outwardly, I assume nothing has seemed amiss, but I'm unaccustomed to such surprises as I had this afternoon, and between that and Paisley's strange energy when we returned, and now Rosalie, I still feel quite ruffled.

This stops Rosalie cold, though. "I wonder why."

"What's wrong? It's one of my favorite dresses."

"Great-Aunt Gertrude detests pink," she says, and then Paul calls to her from the doorway and she hurries away, and Rafe comes to collect me.

"What's wrong?" he says, when he sees my face, and I can only laugh. What a ridiculous situation.

"I've been informed that Great-Aunt Gertrude doesn't like pink," I say, composing myself.

"I've never heard that," he says, frowning. "Though I guess maybe she wouldn't think to tell me something like that."

"No, I suppose not."

Rafe takes my hand, gives it a little squeeze. "Anyway, it's not like it matters, right? Nothin' to get worked up about. Though I appreciate you're taking it so seriously."

"You know, you're right. I just got so caught up." He smiles down at me, and I can't help but smile back.

"She isn't here yet, if you want to go change anyway."

"I do not want to go change, I love this dress."

He shrugs. "Then wear it." People outside are shouting his name. I'm given to understand tonight's party is a lot of rodeo friends, and some other local friends, both of the business sort and the high school sort. "That's our cue." He holds out his arm and I take it, and we walk outside to applause and a few whistles. Somebody pops a bottle of champagne, and then another, and tall glasses, sparkling in the faerie lights, are passed around. I'm more than accustomed to plunging into a crowd of strangers as though I belong, and these are exceedingly welcoming strangers, all eager to meet Rafe's very sudden lady love at long last.

Great-Aunt Gertrude has not yet appeared when Rosalie appears at my elbow with an umbrella drink. "Here, you're running low," she says. "They're Paisley's specialty."

"Oh, thank you, I need this! My throat is dry with so much talking." I take a moment to admire the colors. "A Tequila sunrise? Is it the wrong time of day?"

"It's sunrise somewhere, probably," one of the nearby rodeo people observes, and we all laugh.

"They're always really good," Rosalie says, as I take my first sip.

"It isn't my usual cocktail, but it is lovely," I say. One can't drink champagne all the time, after all.

"I really like them," Rosalie says, but she doesn't have one, and I wonder if the news that Bits was going to share earlier was a reason Rosalie would opt not to consume alcohol at this party. I see Paisley across the crowd and raise my drink to her, just a little, and she smiles and winks at me before returning to her conversation, and I return to mine.

They're telling me a very tamed but still hair raising rodeo story about Rafe when Gabe finds me. "Hey, R.J. just got the news, Great-Aunt Gertrude isn't coming tonight after all," he says.

"Waiting for Great-Aunt Gertrude, a sequel play by Samuel Beckett," I say, and giggle. He frowns and looks at me, cocking his head.

"What?"

"It's a theater joke, darling, it's all right." I set down my empty glass on a passing server's tray, and they don't even break stride.

He shrugs. "Sorry, not really my thing."

"Where *is* Rafe?" I ask. Am I speaking too loudly? I should probably have spent more time with him tonight publicly. But these are his friends, that is how parties go.

"Some of the girls wanted to see the baby ostriches, so he took them over to the nursery." I should have asked for that. But everybody here will assume I would have already been. Baby ostriches indeed, I'm certain they're horrifyingly ugly. Everybody here is about babies, it's so very odd.

Gabe goes away again while I'm woolgathering, and my rodeo people seem to have also disappeared, and I realize that the crowd and the fairy lights have become a multicolored smear as if I was back on the carousel. I am not drunk; I have not drunk enough for this, and this is not what drunkenness feels like, and there are many reasons I am not given to dwelling on the past, but it puts me in mind of my fairly recent private stay at an unnamed government facility, I take a few steps, but I'm not sure where I intend to go, and stumble into the little fence that surrounds the pool. This is embarrassing, I think, though I do not feel embarrassed. I feel as though the part of me that controls everything has detached, and the part of me that takes action is a floating balloon, and somehow I manage to coordinate the two and fumble in my bracelets and find my panic button. It doesn't make any noise when I press it. Did I press it correctly? It doesn't light up, either, but I suppose that would defeat the purpose of secretly having a panic button, if it had any outward appearance of such.

"Madison, honey, are you okay? You don't look so good." Paisley, sweet and far too solicitous, is at my elbow. It seems as though I can't really see her face. I wish I still had my glass, I was so foolish. It's because she sent Rosalie. It's because I was distracted from Lorraine earlier, or this never would have happened. Wouldn't she be shocked if I slapped her pretty face? But I can't organize myself or marshal my senses to do so, or to rebuff her, and just grip onto the fence with my wooden-feeling hands, like they're puppet hands, the sort where each finger has its own little joints all the way down to the tips. She takes me by the shoulders, gently but firmly, and says "Let's get you out of here." I can't let go of the fence, though, and don't think

I should like to go with her, though I can't sort out why that would be. After all, hasn't she been so kind and welcoming? Haven't we had so many parties together already? "Madison, come on now." Her tone becomes more brusque, businesslike, and just like that, my hands fall open.

It's a little too abrupt, and I giggle as she staggers under my sudden full weight. Serves her right, is this her fault? I'm not drunk, I'm not. I don't know where the house is, but I'm also not convinced that's where she is trying to take me, and I don't want to go with her, and simply sit down right there on the pavement. It feels nice and cool, and suddenly I feel flushed all over, and so the next reasonable step is to lie down, pillowing my cheek on the nice smooth-rough concrete that glitters just a little in the party lights. It's more comfortable than I might have thought, but when, if ever, have I just laid on pavement? I think perhaps never.

Paisley tries again to get me to my feet, her tone complaining but her words have gone away somewhere, and then her voice sharpens, far too high pitched, and I don't like that, I can't abide high pitched noises. I can't seem to put my hands over my ears, so I squinch my eyes closed instead. There are other voices, all smeared like the lights were, and somebody gets me up off the pavement in a strong, sure motion but now that my eyes are closed I can't open them again, but I know that it isn't Paisley. There's no mistaking the feel of the skin on Dolly's fake hand no matter what any marketing material says. And she always smells a little like gun oil. I'm leaning on that arm that I can mostly ignore otherwise, and that I never mention, because I don't want her to feel bad, or to think that I think ill of her for having it. But I'm safe from Paisley, and that's enough for me.

Chapter Eleven

I wake up in that long blue hour of the morning before dawn, my mouth the driest it has ever in my life been, feeling as though, physically, my cheeks are just stuffed to bursting with cotton. They are not, of course. I'm lying in an unaccustomed way and shift on the bed, my skirt wrapping around my legs. Bed? Skirt? I have very blurry, sudden memories of the party, the pavement, and feel a surge of panic that whatever I was drugged with didn't properly let me feel at the time. Ketamine, probably. Funny, the law enforcement and animal husbandry overlap. I'm not used to fully panicking either, though, and don't quite know what to do with myself once I sit up, gasping. Am I about to cry? I examine the feeling with fascination.

In the gap between my action and reaction, Dolly gets out of the chair she was in, back against the closed door. I know she can move quickly, maybe even more quickly than I've seen, but she approaches me with surprising care, perhaps as one would a distressed animal. "Hey, Bristol, how you feeling?"

"Very thirsty," I say slowly, to make sure I can. My eyelashes are gummy with the mascara I didn't wash off last evening. My hair has come only partly undone, the very ends of it tickling my neck. My shoes are off, but otherwise I'm still dressed.

"Hold on a sec." She goes into the bathroom, runs the water. She hasn't turned on any lights, and I can't remember if she's had that dreadful eye surgery or not. Perhaps she's just always had good vision in different environments. "Here."

"Thank you," I say, and then would have promptly spilled the water into my lap if she did not reach out and steady my hand. My hands are very cold, it seems.

"Just take it easy," she says, taking the glass once I've drained it. "You should probably sleep more." Had I been sleeping? It could be considered sleep. I blink at her, not really knowing what to say. "I'm not leaving," she says, and that must have been what I was waiting for. I lay my head on the pillow and slip away once more, as she pulls a blanket up around my shoulders.

When next I awaken, it is much more calmly. The room is *very* bright. I only open my eyes at first, I don't thrash about or jerk upright, and Dolly remains slouched dozing in her chair against the door until I actually move. I do try to be slow and quiet, I imagine she did not get sufficient sleep last night, or at least not very restful sleep, upright in a wingback chair dragged over from elsewhere in the room. But she's too sensitive, something I did not anticipate, and is awake immediately.

"Morning, sunshine," she says, uncrossing her legs and sitting up.

"Good morning," I say. I feel oh so much better, my thoughts and actions in line once again. I hate that feeling, that detachment and removal from myself. That loss of control.

"I'll clear outta here so you can get cleaned up." She stands and stretches, and some unnamed part of her crackles. "Your phone was going nuts, but it can probably wait."

"I'm sure it was," I say, pulling the pins out of my hair, or rather, the pins that were left out of my hair. What a dreadful night. "Dolly, what—"

"Not now, go get hosed off." She moves the chair back to where it was and exits the room, whistling.

My phone does have ever so many messages, and I glance at them and then set it aside. It isn't necessary to face them immediately, and indeed, I would benefit from waiting. I ache all over, and a long and steaming shower eventually banishes that, as I use every potion, lotion, and ointment that I've got at my disposal. What a positively dreadful night. I wasn't sure of all that had happened; if I was, I would have an idea of my actions moving forward. As it is, I have nothing satisfying to concentrate on, just loose ends and partial clues, and I make an effort to clear my mind instead.

Towel-wrapped, I survey my clothing. The pink dress isn't too worse for wear, it just needs to be dry-cleaned. The dress I select for the day is light blue, patterned subtly with silver stars that shift in the light, appearing and disappearing. I dry my hair and pin it up sleekly, do my makeup lightly but with care. A single night sleeping in makeup won't do too much damage. I finish off the look with some minimalist silver jewelry, slip into a pair of heels, and then finally I am ready to face the world, and go to join Bits and Dolly in the suite's sitting room.

Dolly is mixing up something at the mini bar, perhaps a hangover cure. Never in my life have I needed such a thing, though this obviously isn't the usual sort of hangover. I check in with myself; I'm still feeling very bewildered, and exceedingly angry.

"What's the plan?" Bits asks after looking at me for a moment.

"Obviously, I want to know what happened. And then I want them to regret that. Most specifically Paisley."

"Apparently there's a long history of kidnapping the Sutter bride, as I found out when R.J. was bawling Paisley out in front of everybody gathered, and I was handling you." Dolly pauses a moment in her mixing. "It really was a sight, she wasn't ready for him to correct her at all, much less in full voice and in public. I guess he'd already told her in what he assumed to be no uncertain terms that they wouldn't be doin' the kidnapping thing with you, no way, no how."

"Kidnapping," I say faintly. Obviously, nobody here but Bits and Dolly have any inkling of what sort of effect such an event, however in fun, may have on me. I think I also still perhaps have some baggage to work through with regards to my recent experience, even though it is done with. It's so unfair, to still be emotionally caught up with it.

I take a deep breath, but before I can continue, Dolly says "Is it still kidnapping when it's an adult? It seems like that'd be sort of a champagne thing."

I look at her. Heaven help me, I somewhat grasp what she means. "Dolly, no, it's—"

"Like it's only kidnapping between the ages of nothin' and seventeen, and after that it's sparkling abduction?" She laughs loudly, and hands me what looks like a mimosa. She's still wearing her bodyguard clothing from last night, while Bits is more normally dressed. I can't help but also laugh. I take the drink and settle into a chair with a sigh.

"No, it's. It's still kidnapping," Bits says, eyebrows quirked.

"The woman is a jealous menace," I say, sipping the drink after a split second's hesitation that I push past. I can trust Dolly. It *is* a mimosa, though there's something else in it. Pineapple juice. It's lovely.

"She is," Dolly says. "So we gotta put the fear of god in her, then."

"It's probably the option that's kindest to Rafe, since ruining his friend's livelihood and portfolios is likely to distress him." Or worse; it isn't often that I in fact want to do bodily harm to a person, but it also isn't often that I myself am threatened with the implication of bodily harm.

"And he was willing to go to bat in your honor. If I hadn't whisked you away, he was gonna."

"He's very sweet," I say thoughtfully. "I do think he'll make some lucky lady very happy one day."

"But not you," Dolly says.

"No, not me. What, did you think I was actually falling for him?"

She shrugs. "Well, for almost anybody else in the world, the signs were there. But it's the job, and you're just always real convincing."

"Thank you," I say.

"So, a couple of things," Bits says, and I turn my attention to her. She's been waiting Dolly and I out patiently, as she so often does. "First, somebody, probably Paisley, talked to the gossip columns about last night, and they have an actual good picture of you circulating. Second, I don't know if any other members of agency X are in town, but Will got in last night. Third—"

"This is the one that's gonna be good news, right Bitsy?" Dolly asks, grinning hard and flinty.

"Paisley has been texting R.J. all morning and he's been ignoring her all morning. She's starting to threaten him now with pictures she says she has. I've had a look through her cloud and so far haven't found anything digital, but she takes a lot of pictures."

"Oh, they must be in the safe," I say. "There were a lot of envelopes."

"She just opened her safe in front of you?" Bits asks.

"Yes, it's in her little office or craft room, behind a painting."

"Would she really nuke her own marriage so the guy she broke up with a few years back pays attention to her?" Dolly asks, finally sitting down with her own mimosa.

"Maybe? She doesn't really seem very reasonable."

"I guess when it comes down to it, I'd rather be married to a cowboy than an accountant."

"Retired cowboy," I say.

"Yeah, can't forget the tragic backstory." Dolly laughs, then shakes her head. "Gotta wonder how fun and innocent this little kidnapping schtick was actually gonna be, if the ringleader was willing to open her safe of blackmail material in front of you."

"I'd been trying to avoid wondering," I say stiffly, and she frowns.

"Sorry."

"There's no way any of us could have known," I say after a moment of taut silence. "And I suppose that I need to face Rafe sooner or later."

"You've got every right to just stay in bed today," Bits says. "I can just go tell him that you're okay, but resting."

"Thank you, Bits darling, but I do think I'd rather just face the world."

"Just make sure you hydrate," Dolly says. "Now, I gotta go get myself hosed off."

I'VE ONLY SPENT A HANDFUL of days here, not truly long enough to know where in his home Rafe might be found. I do try some likely places, the breakfast room, and his office, before I find him outside. He's talking to one of the employees who works with the ostriches, but breaks off when he sees me, meets me halfway across the drive. "Madison, I am so fucking sorry about last night, I don't even know where to start."

"It isn't your fault," I say, perhaps a little startled at his vigor.

"No, but I still feel like I should've known Paisley would pull something. She's always pushing boundaries, and doesn't respect what anybody tells her, and I know that. I just thought that she'd listen to me, about this. Or I should've warned you, but like I said, I thought it was settled."

"If she told you it was, you had no reason to doubt her. You've known each other a long time."

"We have. And after it didn't work out with us, and she married Ned, I thought that was it, we were friends, it was done. But I kicked her out last night, and she's not coming to the wedding." He pauses. "I might've told her that I don't care if I ever see her again."

"Rafe!" I'm definitely startled, and a little touched. "I'm sure you don't mean that. After all, I'm only here for a little while longer. You're paying me to do this. There isn't any need to—"

"Well that's just it. She doesn't know I'm paying you to do this. As far as Paisley is concerned, I brought you home after love at first sight, and I'm head over heels for you. And this is what she did."

"You're right," I say, after a pause. We're standing quite close together, talking quietly. I can feel his conflict, that he wants to comfort me, put an arm around me, and also doesn't feel like he should touch me. "You're right, she doesn't know the truth of it. I certainly didn't tell her."

"I just wish I knew what was going on in her head. What a stupid, reckless choice."

"How did she take being ejected from the party? And the invitation rescinded?"

"Oh, she got all doe eyed, and said 'R.J., you know you don't mean that! The wedding is the day after tomorrow!' And I told Ned to get her off my property and out of my sight, and tried to chase after you and your bodyguards, to help, but Darlene there isn't somebody to be tangled with." He shakes his head, rubbing the back of his neck. "What am I supposed to do here? Sorry isn't good enough, do you want a bonus, maybe? Anything like that?"

"I'll consider it and let you know," I say. It is such an impossible situation, but it is a comfort that he's so conflicted about it. Not that I thought he was the sort of man to allow his old friends and ex-fiancée to drug somebody he'd hired just for fun, but I did not expect his unilateral support on the matter. I assumed he would be cross with Paisley but also be inclined to forgive and move on. "Thank you," I say, after perhaps a bit too much time has passed, but he waits for me.

"You're welcome. I wish like hell it just didn't happen, but it did. You're okay? You don't need to go to the doctor or anything?"

"I don't think I need a doctor, no." The worst time to ask if somebody is okay is when they are not; the social convention is to say yes, even when it is not true. "She didn't give me too much, other than that it was without my consent, and I believe it leaves the system quickly."

He lets out a long sigh. "Okay then."

"I do think I want to meet with her, though," I say. "Not at one of our houses, at a cafe perhaps."

"You do? Why?"

"Perhaps to make effort that she never does anything like this again." This will take some time and coordination, though, so that I have her engaged while those pictures are procured. If they truly exist. And then there's Will to think of, but he's a separate problem. Bits likes her programming puzzles, and I like my social ones.

"Well, you want to meet in public, so I guess I don't need to worry about what you'll do to her."

"And I'm not Darlene," I say, smiling sweetly. I wonder if Bits and Dolly have been listening; they've been notably silent.

"That you are not. Not that Darlene isn't perfectly charming, mind. You're just real different."

"We get on well."

"She's loyal to you, that's a fact." The ostrich employee, who had gone away, has returned and is standing at a polite remove. "I'm sorry, I probably ought to—"

"No, it's quite alright. Go about your business, and I'll let you know should anything important happen. Or alarming."

"Yeah, keep me in that loop." We laugh together, a little ruefully, and he lifts my hand and brushes a kiss across my knuckles. "You're a special lady, Madison, I'm glad to have known you."

"Thank you," I say, surprised and touched. "It's such good fortune we met at that party."

"Even after last night?" Oh dear, I do know that look on his face all too well.

"Even after last night, I'd say." I'm perhaps not being entirely truthful, but our relationship hasn't required that.

I return to the suite and devote time to my phone's messages and notifications. One from Marquis, saying to call them when I could. An apology from Rosalie. Other pings from friends who had picked up on the gossip and were shocked to hear of my engagement, and wanted to know if it was actually me. Bits is right; the picture the column has is better than ones they previously had, but still not crystal clear. I wonder if Paisley sent it to them. I've no missives from Paisley. A little short message from Lorraine, who I do not think has seen any fresh gossip column news, but who says it was unbelievably nice to see me again. And I think about how she said that the rodeos were fun.

"Bits darling, what were you going to tell me last night, when Paisley came and whisked me away?"

A brief pause, before she answers from the couch. "Hmm?"

"We were interrupted last night."

"Oh. What I said this morning, that Will was on his way and had motel reservations. He checked in not too long ago. I guess it's to our advantage that he wants to arrest you himself?"

That indeed shortens the post-wedding timeline, if not the pre-wedding one. We spent so much time lazing about, and now everything has come together in a final rush. "And Dolly is...?"

"She said that if you didn't know, you wouldn't have to lie about it." Bits in general avoids eye contact, and right now is no exception. This would normally be very frustrating for me, Dolly going off-script once more, but I perhaps have an inkling of what she might do. I hope.

"Just so," I say, instead of any of the expected responses, and Bits' eyes dart to mine. "I'm going to invite Paisley out to a cafe, I think. I expect you or Dolly to send me a useful message at some point during that tête-à-tête, does that sound correct?"

"I'd say so, yeah."

"We understand each other, then." I send Paisley the message, even grandly suggesting that she might pick the establishment. I check my hair and my makeup, find them satisfactory. "I'm quite surprised you did not accompany Dolly."

"I slow her down," Bits says ruefully.

"Don't we all."

My phone chimes; Paisley has sent me an address.

Chapter Twelve

Because I prefer to be driven does not mean that I cannot drive, but Paisley still seems surprised to see me park in front of the cafe and walk to her table alone. "Surprised you don't still have your bodyguards," she says, a bit snidely. The implication being that they didn't help me all that much last night, except that they did. It really is testament to Dolly's restraint that Paisley is upright and able to maintain this attitude, I'm quite surprised and impressed. Dare I say proud?

"They're occupied elsewhere," I say airily. "I'll go order, and be with you directly."

"I thought about getting you something, but..." She smirks and sips her iced tea. The gloves are off, I see.

"Oh don't be silly, you'd have no idea what I want." I smile and sweep up to the counter, scanning the kitschy chalked menu as I go. I waver briefly between an espresso and an affogato, but it is quite warm out and I do think the affogato will be far more refreshing. And Paisley, indeed, regards my glass with obvious surprise when I return to the table and settle myself across from her.

"Well you made quite the scene last night," she says.

"I suppose I did; ketamine isn't my party drug of choice, I'm afraid, even if the drink you made me did taste lovely otherwise." I spoon up some of my espresso-drowned ice cream and regard her with the full weight of my disdain.

She makes a show of confusion, quirking her lips and furrowing her brow, setting her drink down. "I'm sure I don't—"

I cut her off. "There are tests for chemicals in drinks, I'm very certain you realize that. And when people very suddenly behave out of character, well..."

"You're a stranger, how would we know your character?" She says, not quite maintaining her lightness of tone.

"You made me feel so *welcome*." I shake my head, sip my drink. "And then do this ugly, awful thing. I'm not certain what your aim was, Paisley." I pause as though I want to hear her answer, and when she takes a breath to speak, I lean in just slightly and say "He doesn't want you, darling. He will never again be yours."

She jerks back in her seat as though I've slapped her, getting red across the cheekbones and white around the lips. "How dare you," she says slowly, and with deliberation. "You don't even know him. You waltz in here like you're hot shit, like you *belong* here, and I never even heard of you before last week. Never laid eyes on you. Never had the slightest notion that R.J. had somebody he was interested in, much less interested in *marrying*. And you want to be treated like you're family? Like we *want* you?"

"Truly, your opinion doesn't matter. We do not require your input." She's breathing in short, furious little bursts now. I must be careful to bait her only far enough, not into actually flinging herself across the table at me. Though I am confident I could handle her. I pause, and then soften my voice into a pitying tone. "Paisley, just be happy with what you have. I see how

Ned looks at you. I'm not certain what you thought you still had with Rafe, but even though some flame was once there, it has long since gone out. You need to let it go. You can't possibly hope to go on like this." The change in her expression is exquisite. She goes from even more incandescently furious to smug again. Cat who swallowed the canary smug, just as I'd hoped.

Glowing now but happily, triumphant, Paisley says "Oh, but that's where you're wrong, *darling*. I have proof that R.J. still loves me, or is at least interested enough to do the deed. And we both know how he is, what a white knight. He won't be able to help but step in and protect me from Ned, who is sure to be angry, and jealous. There's just no telling what—" My phone chimes once, twice, thrice, and I smile, raising my eyebrows just a little before I look away from her entirely and retrieve my phone from my purse as it pings again.

I unlock the screen, to three photographs and a video. The photographs are of the open safe, Dolly holding an envelope marked "R.J. at the Point Inn," and a number of polaroids fanned like a hand of cards, of Paisley and a man, anyway, in flagrante delicto. The video is Dolly walking out of the office and onto the adjoining screened porch, lighting the photographs with the engraved lighter from Paisley's desk, and dropping them into one of those little metal fire pits once they've burned beyond recognition.

"What are you doing?" Paisley asks.

"You'll want to see these," I say, and she accepts my send request. She swipes through the photos, blinking rapidly, and gets very still when she comes to the video, her mouth growing very pinched. I finish my affogato as she stares at her phone in silence. Dolly really did time things just so, she must have entered Paisley's house not long after Paisley left to meet me here. Then she could crack the safe at her leisure, take care of the photos, and provide me with the grand reveal. We really do work well together, despite our differences.

What does one say, after their blackmail fodder has gone up in smoke? I do wonder who that man at the Point Inn was; it seems unlikely for it to have been Rafe. I *do* think Paisley is correct, though, he's the sort of man whose morality would not let a woman be ruined with such a claim. It would have worked. Perhaps they might have even been happy, after a fashion. Clouds are darkening the sky the longer we sit, rain suddenly imminent. Paisley still seems frozen, her castle in the air having crumbled apart before her eyes. I do think the fight has gone out of her; if she was going to come across the table at me, it would have been the moment she realized what she was seeing on her screen.

I dab my lips to make sure no ice cream remains there and stand; she looks at me a little blankly as my chair scrapes back. "I'll be sure your hair combs are returned to you," I say, and she gives a single dazed nod. I wonder if she will cry here, or in the car, or once she's home. I wonder if she'll ever tell Ned, and I wonder what she may have told Ned already, if she thought this was a sure thing.

The first raindrops patter onto the pavement around me as I walk to the car. There are people who talk about the scent of rain on the earth, but one of my pleasures is the smell of rain on hot pavement. I slide into the driver's seat and lock the doors, settle my purse on the seat beside me.

//It's probably not a crazy coincidence// Bits says //But Will is at the Point Inn.//

"Shall I drop in on him, while I'm out? I was going to wait but I'm not certain that's to our advantage."

//Bristol, the wedding is tomorrow. The rehearsal dinner is later.//

"Yes, and here I am with an unforeseen gap in my schedule." I recall having driven past the Point Inn during our wanderings, and am able to get myself there without much trouble. "What room?"

//17.//

I park next to his rental car and sit a moment, listening to the rain pattering on the roof and hood of the car, watching the pavement steam. I get perfume out of my purse to freshen up, the hyacinth scent that I like to wear when it rains, and that I was wearing when Will and I once sat down together in a very fancy restaurant indeed.

"Be sure to trap the security footage."

//I know how to do my job, Bristol.// Dolly is strangely silent, but it's possible she's also off on her own errand, and we will all regroup this evening after the rehearsal dinner.

I stand in the rain just for a moment, both to bedraggle my hair ever so slightly and also to make sure that the perfume is properly affected, then go and rap lightly on the door to room 17, wooden I think, and painted a pleasant marmalade sort of color. There's a moment of pause, then a shadow crosses the eyehole, and the door is flung open. "Madison," he says with deliberation, trying to mask his surprise. He's wearing the same category of suit that he was when we met previously, midrange, nondescript, dark navy. "Like the avenue, I assume?"

"You clever darling, you do catch on," I say, and he stands aside to allow me inside.

"I saw your picture in the paper," he says, closing the door quickly.

"You're being very generous to that gossip rag," I say, surveying the room for a moment. Two double beds, but only one of them is rumpled with the evidence of somebody having sat upon the bedspread to watch television, an overnight bag on the other. Only one set of toiletries laid upon the bureau: a comb, deodorant, cologne. I pick up the bottle and give it a cursory sniff; something peppery and department store, but serviceable.

"What are you doing here?"

"I was hoping for your help," I say, after letting the silence stretch between us, punctuated by the rain.

"My help?" I wonder if he imagined what our meeting might be like, when he finally caught up to me. He must have. How I would look, where we would be, what he would say. This abrupt invasion of his space is none of those things.

"You saw me in the paper," I say, turning to him now. "One of those dreadful people drugged me. If not for Dolly's help, who knows what may have happened. I might not be standing here talking to you."

"You seem very, uh, intimate with at least one of those dreadful people. He has no idea who you are, does he?"

I smile, slowly. "He doesn't. To be fair, neither do you."

"No, I guess I don't." He sits on the edge of the rumpled bed. "You might as well tell me a story."

Oh, the poor darling, his pride is still wounded. "The marriage is simply a business arrangement, I have no attachment to him."

"There's a surprise." He's had more training, or practice, at outward composure. He seems more self assured. I wonder if he has a gun.

"Do you really think I'm so heartless?" I allow myself to pout, just a little.

"I think that you're very business minded."

"I suppose that's fair." I sit on the edge of the made bed, facing him. There's enough space between that our knees do not touch, quite, but we're close enough that I can feel his warmth. "But of course not everybody was in on the arrangement, so the woman who was to stand in as my maid of honor, and who is also his high school sweetheart and ex-fiancée, thought that she was losing her final chance at happiness with him. Hence last night."

He laughs a little, in surprise or in disbelief. "You get into the wildest situations. Or is that the plot to the world's most popular soap opera, and I just don't know it because I don't watch soap operas?"

"It is a summary of the last week and a half of my life," I say.

"Heavily edited, I assume." I only smile at that, and he sighs and doesn't let the silence last quite so long this time. "So what help do you think I would give you? Oh, I could take you into protective custody, what about that."

"I'm certain you'd like that," I say, shifting my weight a little and holding out my hands, offering my wrists to him. "Do you need to cuff me?"

He reddens then, just like the Will I remember, pushes my hands away just a little and stands up, walks to the bureau to put some space between us. "No, I don't have handcuffs. I'm not going to handcuff you."

"Then why are *you* here? Were you just upset to not be invited to the wedding?"

"I've followed a lot of false leads, trying to find you. I admit, I didn't actually think it was going to be you, here." And neither did his higher-ups, is what I assume he isn't saying. He was free to come and investigate for himself, but they are done assuming that sightings are credible. "I kind of couldn't believe that a paper like that would be right."

"And yet here you are."

"Here I am." He smiles, laughs a little, like he can't believe it worked, and now he doesn't know what to do. He ought to call backup, likely, though how long it would take them to arrive is something I don't know, and Bits would rapidly find out. "And here you are."

"Yes, that does make things rather difficult for you, doesn't it darling," I say. I've put my hands down, but am still sitting on the bed.

"Come again?"

"Well you allowed me into your room so willingly. And I'm not certain what action you are supposed to take, but clearly you haven't yet. There are timestamps on security footage, and there are protocols that agencies follow, even the sort that has you in its employ."

He shakes his head. "I see what you're trying to do. But some decisions are discretionary, nothing that you're saying is all that damning."

"Oh, I see." I don't know if I believe him, but he's still a bit flustered over the handcuffs business, and that might be muddying the waters. "Perhaps I'm on the wrong trail, assuming you want to arrest me anyway. Perhaps you're here to recruit me instead. Tell me that my skills would be well suited in your organization, and that you can offer amnesty for our past encounters."

"Is that what you think?"

I smile, tilt my head. "No, but it's a pretty story. And you did ask for a story."

"You're right, I did." Now that he's standing, he doesn't quite know how to position himself. He ends up leaning against the bureau. I glance at my watch.

"Have someplace to be?"

"The rehearsal dinner," I say. "If you aren't going to be arresting me now, I really ought to—"

"I read your file," he says abruptly, like he's been holding it back this entire time.

"My file?"

"From when you were in Homeland custody." It's to his credit that I wasn't expecting that; I allow my reaction to play across my face before making a show of composing myself once again, and I see the shadow in his eyes. "I'm sorry that happened to you."

"Thank you," I say after a pause and a deep breath that I allow to shake just a little. "It was..." I don't finish my sentence, though; I drop my gaze and sigh.

"Yeah, so. Another reason for no handcuffs."

"I truly do appreciate that," I say, looking up at him, my voice pitched a little more quietly, and for the second time today, I see a certain type of look cross a man's face, and drop my eyes again. I sit very still and quiet, and allow him to assume that I'm struggling to keep composed after being reminded of my harrowing experience.

"So getting married as a business arrangement isn't illegal," he says after several moments.

"Does this mean you're letting me go?"

"I'm probably crazy but. For right this second, yeah, I'm letting you go. Plus I'm sure you have that video of me letting you in here." He gives a self deprecating laugh. "It wouldn't count as a clean arrest."

"I thought you said that some things were discretionary?" I say, teasing a little as I get to my feet.

"I think both of us say a lot of things." We laugh together, what a strange sensation that is.

"When will I see you next?" I ask, as he walks me to the door.

"Before you leave town, hopefully," he says. Not a threat, or a promise, from the sound of it. We have indeed both said a lot of things. He stands in the doorway and watches me get in the car and drive away.

Chapter Thirteen

At the rehearsal dinner, I catch Rosalie when she arrives to tell her that she's now the maid of honor. I hadn't answered any of her messages earlier in the day, and perhaps I should have. It's possible my silence would have prevented her from coming, but to her credit, she's here.

"Madison, I'm so sorry," she says before I can get any words out, and hugs me. I'm so very surprised that I let her, and after a moment, I hug her back. Though I've spent the last little while cultivating what she and everybody here thinks of me, I do wonder what she actually thinks of me. And I wonder what she'll think when I'm gone; will I fade swiftly from her memory, as if I was an imaginary friend or a character in a movie only partly paid mind to? Or have I left enough of a blazing impression that she'll think of me years and decades down the line, perhaps even describe one very strange spring when her friend suddenly brought home a fiancée that nobody had heard of, and just as suddenly, just a few weeks later, she was gone. Goodness, it does sound like a soap opera.

"It's okay, I know it was Paisley," I say. "It has been the entire time. And since she's no longer coming to the wedding, I need you to do a tremendous favor for me, and be my maid of honor."

"Of course I will," she says, pink with surprise, or maybe with the tears that I can see she's struggling to not let fall. I should have tried to spend more time with her, but she required less handling and active manipulation, and so I left her undisturbed.

"Thank you so much, darling, I knew I could count on you."

"Did you see Paisley?" she asks. "She said she was going to talk to you today and then stopped answering my messages."

Blessedly, Rafe calls me from across the room, and I turn to go to him. "I did see her briefly," I say over my shoulder. "I told her I'd make sure she got her hair combs back."

"You were gone a real long time," Rafe says in a low voice once I'm at his side. "Everything okay?"

"I do think so, yes. We're so close now," I say.

"So long as I'm married tomorrow, you won't have to worry about me anymore," he says, seriously because that was why we did all of this in the first place, but conflicted, because he didn't want there to be any kind of a harmful cost. The only thing we were hurting was the intentions of the trust-setters, placing this unnecessary marriage date restriction on his inheritance. I realize I've never asked who came up with that; his parents, presumably. Or maybe it's another tradition, like the kidnapping of the Sutter bride.

"By this time tomorrow, you'll be married," I say in a less confidential tone, smiling. "You're not nervous are you?"

He laughs, surprised. People near us look around, and smile at the presumably happy couple sharing a moment. "Nervous? Nah. I've ridden some of the meanest bulls in the world, and been thrown by some of the meanest bulls in the world. Marriage isn't going to match up to that."

"I'm sure you're right," I say.

"I know we're going to be busy tomorrow, so I guess I want to say this now, even though we're not exactly alone," he says, lowering his voice again. "But I think I'm really going to miss you."

"Rafe," I say, touched, and he brushes a kiss on my cheek and we get on with the rehearsal dinner, which is far more dinner than rehearsal. Everybody knows how to walk down the aisle, even if they've never done it before themselves. Gabe stands in for the judge, whom we'll meet tomorrow at the event, and we do a single short runthrough there in the dining hall before the appetizers start coming out.

At one point, I glance up and notice Dolly standing in one of the open doors to the verandah. She's in the midst of lighting a cigarette, and as she snaps an engraved bronze lighter closed, she sees me looking and grins before wandering off so that the smoke doesn't get inside. Bits doesn't make an appearance, but I can assume that she's on the chaise in the master suite, keeping digital tabs on everything, and making arrangements for our imminent exit. There are digital footprints that we will want swept away, caches cleared, impressions erased, and the sooner she starts, the sooner we will be done. Besides needing to pay attention to the Agency X aspect of things now, though I do think Will shall be on very good behavior. I could be incorrect.

It's a fun evening, perhaps even more fun for Paisley's absence. Nobody asks after her, in my earshot; either they were at the party last night and saw the finale, or they saw the paper, or they were already informed by guests who are in the know.

Though nobody but Rafe knows it, this is my farewell dinner here, and I circulate amongst the guests with a flute of champagne and make sure to speak to everybody at least a little bit. I'm not a person who exists here, not really, but I do still want them to think well of me when I'm gone.

At one point, Rosalie says to me "I honestly don't know why we put up with her. I guess we're just used to it."

"It can be hard, handling an old friend's habits," I say.

"Sometimes it takes a new friend to make you realize the way things are."

"Yes, I think it does."

As the evening winds down, and I think some guests have left already, Gabe stands up and shouts "I want to propose a toast."

Rafe and I look at each other from across the room, and he shrugs helplessly. He has no idea what his brother is about. Some of the guests say "toast, toast," surprised, but enthusiastic, and Gabe waits for them to settle down again.

"I know maybe I should save some of this for the best man speech tomorrow," Gabe says. "But what's a rehearsal dinner for if you don't get to practice stuff, right? I want to practice making a speech. I never made a speech before." He isn't slurring, but I do think perhaps he has drunk too much. He pauses, perhaps remembering that a toast and a speech are not the same thing, and weighing one against the other.

"To R.J. and Madison," Rosalie speaks up, holding her glass aloft.

"Hear, hear, to R.J. and Madison," Gabe repeats. Everybody holds up their glasses, and then takes a drink. "I don't know if I've ever seen my brother happier. Not as an adult. Being kids and getting our first cars is a close second." Everybody laughs, and drinks again, and the evening moves to a close.

"I thought we were in trouble there," R.J. teases as Gabe finds his way to us.

"Well, if I actually brought my damn speech notes, maybe you would've been," Gabe says, then laughs. "Nah, nothing bad to say. I don't need to talk about all the times we kicked each other's asses growing up." He laughs again. "Okay maybe I'm a little pissed I didn't see her first, but that ain't really appropriate wedding conversation."

"You're right," Rafe says, and Gabe looks at me.

"Sorry, Madison, I oughtn't have said that."

"It's okay, Gabe."

"See, she calls me the right name. Will you call him R.J. just once?"

I wrinkle my nose ever so slightly. "I fail to see why I would."

Gabe laughs again. "See, she's great. I'm so happy for you two."

Rafe laughs too. "Well thanks. Keep that energy for tomorrow, okay?"

"You know I will." Gabe punches him in the shoulder, gently, and ambles off.

Once the guests have gone, Rafe and I remain outside under the stars for a time. "I suppose we ought to get some sleep before the big day," I say eventually.

"I suppose," he says. "You know. You've been here all this time, and I don't think you've come to see the birds once. Do you want to?"

"See the birds? Certainly not, though I appreciate you've checked in to see."

"Anytime." I've spent just enough time with him, I can imagine his smile.

Dolly and Bits are both waiting for me back in the suite. "Will hasn't called anybody or sent out any messages," Bits says without preamble.

"Did we expect him to?" I ask.

"I didn't expect him not to, that's for sure." She pauses a moment, either parsing what she wants to say next or taking in the latest datastream, it's hard to discern which. "Paisley also hasn't done much. Went home. Screamed at Ned. Threw stuff around."

"Is that all? She's rather predictable, isn't she."

"That's cold, Bristles," Dolly says, but she's grinning.

"Did you take any other souvenirs?" I ask her pointedly.

"Maybe a coupla things. Haven't you always wanted your very own gold ingot?" She tosses it to me abruptly, though not so hard that it would do damage if I didn't catch it. I do catch it, and turn it over in my hands.

"Isn't it funny, how gold is so *heavy* when it's this size? It doesn't seem as though it would be." It's truly a marvel.

"Get yourself somebody who looks at you the way Bristles looks at valuables." Dolly laughs. "Anyway, this has been like a vacation for me. Using the gym, including a pro mechanical bull. I didn't even have to shoot anybody, or hit anybody, though it was real close with Paisley. So thanks, you two, for doing the heavy lifting."

"We all played our parts," Bits says judiciously.

"I somewhat regret that none of us hit Paisley," I confess. "Isn't that wicked?"

"Nah, it's human. Some people just really ought to be hit."

"*Dolly*." But I can't help but laugh, and Bits is laughing too, and I've certainly never seen Bits strike anybody in our time together, so it is a truth. Some people just really ought to be hit. "So that's that, then. Just one little bit left and we've got everything neatly wrapped up."

"Yeah, just you gettin' actually married to a guy who seems more and more in love with you every day," Dolly says in an elaborately casual tone.

"You're forgetting we're leaving not long after, as our duty will have been discharged."

"What, no honeymoon?" Dolly asks in mock surprise.

"No reservations have been made," Bits says. "Somebody asked him the other night, and he said that there's too much going on with the farm right now, and they'll go to Mexico or something in the winter."

"Dolly, you're also forgetting that my real name isn't Madison and that I am actually not, in the eyes of the law, getting married to Rafe."

"Don't worry, Stephanie, I won't forget that." She grins at me, and I give a little sniff. "Hey, I'm supposed to be your bodyguard. Paranoia is good, right?"

"It isn't unwarranted. Though what exactly are you paranoid about? We knew this would burn one of my aliases. Do you think he will prevent me from leaving? Is there a basement he's planned to lock me into?"

"I didn't say that. I don't think he has a dungeon or anything, no." She considers a moment, and her expression is serious for once, I'll give her that credit. "I'm just surprised we don't have a contingency plan, is what I'm saying."

"Just in case of the double cross," Bits says helpfully, before I can react. "Which we absolutely don't assume will happen, but—"

I laugh, and Bits stops and blinks at me. "Oh, is that all?" I ask airily.

"What?"

"Darlings, I've already thought of our best exit, we've just been so scattered for the last couple of days, we hadn't discussed it yet."

"Bristol we are literally connected at all—"

"There are some things one prefers to say face to face, wouldn't you say?"

Bits and Dolly look at each other, and then Dolly laughs. "Well okay then. Care to share with the rest of the class?"

Chapter Fourteen

My wedding day dawns beautifully. It is neither too hot nor too cold, and the air and sky are clear, no clouds, no humidity. My breakfast arrives on a tray from the kitchen, to avoid the possibility of the groom seeing the bride ahead of time, and it is accompanied by a bouquet of beautiful, deep pink roses. No note; I can imagine Rafe wavering over that decision. Knowing what this day is supposed to be like, but also knowing the nature of our agreement.

"Tell me I was just in a fugue state when you took care of the flowers and stuff," Dolly says. "Because I don't remember it, but also can't imagine you forgetting."

"Yes, arrangements were made," I say. "You can't possibly be nervous? Honestly, Dolly."

"Just don't want anything to go wrong on your special day," she grins.

I prepare with care, of course. The dress is perfect, just as expected, though also what a relief due to the rush job. For my something new, I wear a perfume that I bought on one of my outings, honeysuckle and sandalwood. For my something old, I have the Sutter jewels, retrieved from the family bank vault and housed in a padded blue velvet case. For my something borrowed, I have Paisley's combs, though it is with mixed feelings that I slide them into my hair. It would be suiting for the Greek tragedy of her personal narrative, should they turn out to be poisoned, and I scratch my scalp with them and perish here in the cheery sunlight streaming through the window. I also have a pearl bracelet from Rosalie that I wear on the wrist opposite from my usual bracelets. And finally, my something blue is a nice pair of shoes that I can wear all day and dance in as necessary; the cowboy boots did seem as though they would be too much, on further reflection.

Rosalie knocks on the suite door when it's time to get in the limo and go to the church, and Bits lets her in. "Rosalie, darling, I'm so glad you're here," I say, giving her a quick hug. "Could you help me with my veil? The girls are indispensable, but this sort of thing..."

"Of course I can! You look amazing, wow."

"Thank you." We smile at each other in the mirror once the veil is settled. "And I love that dress."

"Thank you! I don't remember when I bought it, but I'd never worn it even once, and thought it was as good as any for maid of honor! I've never been anybody's maid of honor before."

"Not even Paisley?"

"No, she had her sister." Rosalie's smile falters just a little and I take one of her hands and give it a squeeze.

"I'm so sorry, I shouldn't have brought her up! Forget that I did."

"It's okay! I shouldn't be making you feel bad on your wedding day!" We both laugh, and the tension dissipates. "You don't think she might..."

"Show up to the wedding? I will say, Darlene wishes she would."

"I think she knows that." We laugh again.

"Are you riding with me in the limo, to the church?"

"I hope so! I told Paul I was, so he's already there by now."

I check the time. "I do think we are ready, and that now is the perfect time to go."

The church is one that the Sutters helped historically to build, and has weathered many years and many storms. It isn't ostentatious, but it isn't really a utilitarian settlement church either, it's mostly wood with some stone. I imagine the trees that they used were very very old indeed, maybe some of the first trees cut down by colonists who came in. I allow Rosalie to get out first, and she goes inside to make sure everybody's in their proper places. Bits and Dolly came in the other car, and already checked to make sure, security wise, things were how we wanted.

//Will isn't here, if you were wondering// Bits says after Rosalie closes the limo door and walks inside.

"I was, thank you," I say quietly. The limo driver is unlikely to pay me any mind, but there isn't any sense in drawing undue attention.

//Or Paisley// Dolly says, with true disappointment in her voice.

"I'm so sorry, darling."

//I'll live. And so will she.//

Rosalie comes back to the church steps and waves at me, and I step out of the limo. One of the event people from the church comes out behind her, holding her bouquet and mine.

"Thank you so much," I say.

"You're welcome. Everything is ready for you, should I signal them to start?"

"Yes, please."

Rosalie and I smile at each other, and at the swell of organ music, she walks in ahead of me. We've truncated the process of coming down the aisle, as nobody is giving me away, and we know no small children about, so no flower girl or ring bearer. Just my maid of honor, and then myself. My groom and his best man already wait at the altar, with the judge, who is also the pastor here, which was an unusual and interesting thing for me to learn. When one hears judge, one does not think of a church wedding, and yet, here we are.

Rafe and Gabe are both grinning widely, and the faces of everybody as they turn to watch me walk up the aisle are so happy. Some bemused, but in general happy. I've met most of them by this point, through the whirlwind days of our supposed engagement. At the front is a wheelchair, and I meet eyes with Great-Aunt Gertrude at last, though ever so briefly. I can see how Paisley would have thought she was so formidable, and I regret her recent ill health. It would have been ever so interesting, getting to know her at least a little bit. As it is, I pause very briefly, and she very obviously looks me up and down, her lips pursed. Then she looks at my face, I raise an eyebrow, and she nods just slightly. I continue to the altar, and hand my bouquet off to Rosalie as Rafe steps over to take my hands, and the judge begins.

It is surreal, to be at a real wedding that you know in your heart is a fake wedding, to see all the expectant friends and family gathered, to have all of the trappings of a real wedding. What a delightful, delicious secret that we have. Though of course there is the final pièce de résistance, and when the judge, as rote, says, "And if there is anybody present who thinks that this couple should not be married, would they please—" a voice rings out from somewhere in the assembly.

"Me! I object!"

There are actual gasps, and I'm thankful for both the veil and the foreknowledge, that my reaction is both obscured and also I can take care to school my face into one of shock rather than amusement as we turn to face our objector. Lorraine, my oldest partner in crime, standing boldly amongst the seated guests.

Rafe, of course, was unprepared, and he gapes at her. I see again the flicker of recognition in his face that he had when he first approached me at the party that night, and I know now that Lorraine was at the local rodeo when he had his last, worst, accident. Did he see her in the crowd there, before his injury? It's possible. Will it make a good story? It absolutely will.

"And who are you?" the judge asks, a little grumpily. I don't think anybody actually objects at weddings, nowadays. I imagine it used to be quite the issue in the olden days. Or maybe it was a strange convention then as well, to ask. Some social rule about asking a question that you expect by rote to be refused, that everybody is party to.

"This woman isn't who she says she is!" She advances to the aisle. "I don't think she's intended any harm, but she's misrepresented herself."

Rafe tears his eyes from her to look at me, questioning, desperately confused. "She's the one you were looking for, the night we met," I say, firmly and carefully. He's a sweet man who deserves happiness, and Lorraine is my oldest friend, and deserves to be lifted out of the gutter. She's enough like me that, if he was genuinely as enamored as he thought he was, perhaps his affections will transfer. Perhaps not. But what a story this makes.

"Is she?" he asks, breathless, as though he can't believe it. Either he's a quick study, or all of my guesses have been correct. He turns to her, walks down off of the altar to look at her face. "She is," he says, louder and in a more sure tone. A part of me wishes that Will *was* here, in order to witness this ridiculous, over the top scene, which was so carefully crafted.

"What?" Rosalie says behind me, and I glance at her guileless face. She's in complete disbelief.

There's some indistinct whispering in the pews, and Lorraine walks up the aisle and Rafe walks down, and they meet part way. They speak to one another quietly for a few moments, and then he shakes his head and laughs. I can still see Lorraine's face, and she's smiling. He takes her hand and looks around the church, and then looks up at me. "Madison, I think you're right. I think I got so focused on some things that we made a mistake," he says.

"I do think it seems that way, yes," I say. Gabe, still across the altar from me, laughs.

"Well now what?" he asks. "What do you say, judge, can we just change the names on the marriage license or what?" Bless him. I look at Rafe, and then turn to the judge, whose face I would mostly describe as impatient.

"Yes, is that possible?" I ask.

He looks at his watch and sighs. He must have plans right after the ceremony that he needs to get away to. "There's no waiting period here between having a marriage license and the ceremony, so while we won't cross the names off, we can get a new one issued and proceed."

"Is that what you want?" Rafe asks Lorraine, and she smiles and nods, as though she's so overcome that she can't really speak.

"I'll make a call," the judge says, and walks off.

"Madison what...what just happened?" Rosalie asks, barely touching my elbow with the tips of her fingers. She seems quite shaken, actually, and I am sorry that I've been so disruptive to her little world. Though maybe, once all has settled, things will have worked out for the better.

"In a nutshell, I'd say that what happened was love at first sight, except Lorraine is who Rafe saw first." She nods, because she thinks that's what I've expected of her, but I'm not certain she quite grasps the story just yet.

It's then that I think to look at Great-Aunt Gertrude; she's of advanced age and has been in poor health lately, I do hope that this hasn't been too much of a shock for her. But she has a look on her face that is something like delight, as if this is the most fun she's seen or had in quite a long time. She sees me looking at her, makes eye contact, and then her eyes drop, very pointedly, to the Sutter jewels around my neck. I'd be lying if I said I hadn't considered making off with them, but their assessed value is such that it is far more important to me to pull off this social situation. The payment for that, and what Dolly purloined from Paisley's safe, are more than enough.

"Lorraine!" I call, not shouting, but pitched to cut through the murmur of the crowd. She turns to me immediately, and I beckon to her. She says something to Rafe, who bends his head to her to listen, and then sneaks a kiss. She's flushed quite prettily when she comes over to me. "I'm wearing the Sutter jewels," I say to her, and her eyes widen with the realization.

"Oh! Well we should..."

"Let's just go to the ladies room, and swap what we need to," I say. "Your dress is quite nice, but not a wedding dress." No matter her financial situation, Lorraine has always had a fantastic eye for fashion, and has also been handy with a needle. The dress is grass green, with an a-line skirt and ruched bodice. Maybe better suited for a cookout than a church wedding. We trade dresses, giggling a little at the thrill, and at how ridiculous this all is. And how familiar, like when we used to cram into a dressing room together.

"Am I really getting married to R.J. Sutter?" she asks, as I settle her veil and slide Paisley's combs into her hair. I pull the engagement ring off my finger, and hand it to her.

"You really are," I say. "If it's what you want."

She nods, taking the earrings from me, and turning around so I can clasp the necklace. "It is what I want. I don't really know when I got interested in rodeos, and when I started watching, but when I told you that I moved here because I could be poor anywhere, he was part of the reason. I just never dreamed..." She trails off, looking at herself in the mirror.

"You look beautiful," I say.

"You're not going to forget me this time, are you?" she asks, still looking at herself in the mirror.

"I already promised that I would not."

"You promise a lot of things," she says, and we both laugh.

"I confess, I've been caught."

There's a knock at the door, but Dolly doesn't wait for us to answer. "Are you about ready? The judge's clerk or whoever just got here and needs to see IDs and stuff. No blood test at least."

"We'll be out directly," I say.

"I'll tell 'em."

"Do you want my shoes?" I ask Lorraine. "I can't remember, are we the same size there as well?"

Lorraine looks at me critically. "We are, and yes, I'd better take them. Mine are new too, and that blue doesn't go with that dress anyway."

And with that, we are ready, and exit the ladies' room once more. Almost immediately, Lorraine is whisked away to Rafe's side, and embroiled in paperwork and general activity; most of the guests have remained seated or at least amongst the pews, though they're all speaking in full voice, trying to make sense of everything. Rafe looks up one last time, and I blow him a kiss before I slip out the door and walk to the car.

"You've made sure to pack everything?" I ask, even though we all worked together in the suite to do so the night before.

"Of course we did," Dolly says, sliding her sunglasses on and pulling away down the church drive.

"And Bits—"

"I started making sure you'd be a surveillance ghost from the second we got here," she says.

"So sorry to be so bossy, darlings," I say, settling back into the seat.

"Nah, it's fine, you're coming down from being the lady of the house," Dolly says. "We're lucky you didn't pull this with a prince or something."

"Maybe next time," Bits says.

Epilogue

It is not raining when Will next opens his motel door to me. I do not know who he was expecting to be here, but he's unable to hide his surprise when he sees me. "You wanted to see me before I left town," I say, brushing past him into the room.

"I did," he says. He looks pointedly at my bare hands. "The romance didn't work out?"

"It did," I say. "Just not for me."

"You're unbelievable."

"I've been told." His belongings are packed; the comb and things are no longer on the bureau, and his suitcase and briefcase are on the made bed. "I'm surprised you didn't try to make the wedding."

"I wasn't authorized," he says with a frown in his voice. "This was ruled not a credible sighting. It seems Bits does unbelievable work."

"I would agree with that, yes, she does. And after all, one blonde does look very much like another." I smile at him in the mirror and reach into my purse for my lipstick.

He moves to me quickly, catching me by the wrist. "We won't be kissing goodbye this time," he says. Regardless of what was said between us last time, he is reaching for his handcuffs.

Dolly says, if somebody has hold of you like this, to try and touch elbows. I do, opening his hand, and when I reach into my purse next, I pull out a bottle of perfume.

"I'm disappointed you'd think I would perform the same stunt twice," I say, smiling as I remove the cap.

"You understand my caution," he says. He's standing between me and the door, and still thinks he has the upper hand.

"Of course I do," I say, and spray him in the face with Dolly's surplus pepper spray. Then I scoop up his briefcase and step briskly over him to leave the room before I feel the effects of the spray too badly myself.

Jennifer R. Donohue grew up at the Jersey Shore and now lives in central New York with her husband and their Doberman. Though she got a bachelor's degree in psychology, she has always wanted to write. She currently works at her local public library, where she also facilitates a writing workshop. Her work has appeared in Daily Science Fiction, Syntax & Salt, Escape Pod, Truancy, Apex and elsewhere. She blogs at Authorized Musings, where she shares fiction and the tribulations of the writing life, and tweets @AuthorizedMusin.